★ One of the first no~~~~ ~~~~ ~~~~
or not mentioned as ~~~~
to it's female auth~~~~

THE HISTORY OF T~~~~

The Fair Vow-br~~~~

Aphra Behn

Some key themes:

- women's desire.
- guilt
- Reputation

• Isabella's desire to uphold society's
~~st~~ expectations of being a virtuous
woman, her love for Henault after
breaking her vows, but also her
desire to get away with murder
and to maintain her reputation.
- Wikipedia.

• Using amatory fiction as a way
to write about women.

• The moral being the danger of
vow breaking.

1

THE HISTORY OF THE NUN

Of all the sins, incident to Human Nature, there is none, of which Heaven has took so particular, visible, and frequent Notice, and Revenge, as on that of *Violated Vows*, which never go unpunished; and the *Cupids* may boast what they will, for the encouragement of their Trade of Love, that Heaven never takes cognisance of Lovers broken Vows and Oaths, and that 'tis the only Perjury that escapes the Anger of the *Gods*; But I verily believe, if it were search'd into, we should find these frequent Perjuries, that pass in the World for so many Gallantries only, to be the occasion of so many unhappy Marriages, and the cause of all those Misfortunes, which are so frequent to the Nuptiall'd Pair. For not one of a Thousand, but, either on his side, or on hers, has been perjur'd, and broke Vows made to some fond believing Wretch, whom they have abandon'd and undone. What Man that does not boast of the Numbers he has thus ruin'd, and, who does not glory in the shameful Triumph? Nay, what Woman, almost, has not a pleasure in Deceiving, taught, perhaps, at first, by some dear false one, who had fatally instructed her Youth in an Art she ever after practis'd, in Revenge on all those she could be too hard for, and conquer at their own Weapons? For, without all dispute, Women are by Nature more Constant and Just, than Men, and did not their first Lovers teach them the trick of Change, they would be *Doves*, that would never quit their Mate, and, like *Indian* Wives, would leap alive into the Graves of their deceased Lovers, and be buried quick with 'em. But Customs of Countries change even Nature her self, and long Habit takes her place: The Women are taught, by the Lives of the Men, to live up to all their Vices, and are become almost as inconstant; and 'tis but Modesty that makes the difference, and, hardly, inclination; so deprav'd the nicest Appetites grow in time, by bad Examples.

But, as there are degrees of Vows, so there are degrees of Punishments for Vows, there are solemn Matrimonial Vows, such as contract and are the most effectual Marriage, and have the most reason to be so; there are a thousand Vows and Friendships, that pass between Man and Man, on a thousand Occasions; but there is another Vow, call'd a *Sacred Vow*, made to God only; and, by which, we oblige our selves eternally to serve him with all Chastity and Devotion: This Vow is only taken, and made, by those that enter into Holy Orders, and, of all broken Vows, these are those, that receive the most severe and notorious Revenges of God; and I am almost certain, there is not one Example to be produc'd in the World, where Perjuries of this nature have past unpunish'd, nay, that have not been persu'd with the greatest and most rigorous of Punishments. I could my self, of my own knowledge, give an hundred Examples of the fatal Consequences of the Violation of Sacred Vows; and who ever make it their business, and are curious in the search of such Misfortunes, shall find, as I say, that they never go unregarded.

The young Beauty therefore, who dedicates her self to Heaven, and weds her self for ever to the service of God, ought, first, very well to consider the Self-denial she is going to put upon her youth, her fickle faithless deceiving Youth, of one Opinion to day, and of another

Different types of vows[2]
- Matrimonial vows
- Holy vows, to God.

to morrow; like Flowers, which never remain in one state or fashion, but bud to day, and blow by insensible degrees, and decay as imperceptibly. The Resolution, we promise, and believe we shall maintain, is not in our power, and nothing is so deceitful as human Hearts.

I once was design'd an humble Votary in the House of Devotion, but fancying my self not endu'd with an obstinacy of Mind, great enough to secure me from the Efforts and Vanities of the World, I rather chose to deny my self that Content I could not certainly promise my self, than to languish (as I have seen some do) in a certain Affliction; tho' possibly, since, I have sufficiently bewailed that mistaken and inconsiderate Approbation and Preference of the false ungrateful World, (full of nothing but Nonsense, Noise, false Notions, and Contradiction) before the Innocence and Quiet of a Cloyster; nevertheless, I could wish, for the prevention of abundance of Mischiefs and Miseries, that Nunneries and Marriages were not to be enter'd into, 'till the Maid, so destin'd, were of a mature Age to make her own Choice; and that Parents would not make use of their justly assum'd Authority to compel their Children, neither to the one or the other; but since I cannot alter Custom, nor shall ever be allow'd to make new Laws, or rectify the old ones, I must leave the Young Nuns inclos'd to their best Endeavours, of making a Virtue of Necessity; and the young Wives, to make the best of a bad Market.

In *Iper*, a Town, not long since, in the Dominions of the King of *Spain*, and now in possession of the King of *France*, there liv'd a Man of Quality, of a considerable Fortune, call'd, Count *Henrick de Vallary*, who had a very beautiful Lady, by whom, he had one Daughter, call'd *Isabella*, whose Mother dying when she was about two years old to the unspeakable Grief of the Count, her Husband, he resolv'd never to partake of any Pleasure more, that this transitory World could court him with, but determin'd, with himself, to dedicate his Youth, and future Days, to Heaven, and to take upon him Holy Orders; and, without considering, that, possibly, the young *Isabella*, when she grew to Woman, might have Sentiments contrary to those that now possess him, he design'd she should also become a Nun; However, he was not so positive in that Resolution, as to put the matter wholly out of her Choice, but divided his Estate; one half he carried with him to the Monastery of *Jesuits*, of which number, he became one; and the other half, he gave with *Isabella*, to the Monastery, of which, his only Sister was Lady *Abbess*, of the Order of St. *Augustine*; but so he ordered the matter, that if, at the Age of Thirteen, *Isabella* had not a mind to take Orders, or that the Lady *Abbess* found her Inclination averse to a Monastick Life, she should have such a proportion of the Revenue, as should be fit to marry her to a Noble Man, and left it to the discretion of the Lady *Abbess*, who was a Lady of known Piety, and admirable strictness of Life, and so nearly related to *Isabella*, that there was no doubt made of her Integrity and Justice.

The little *Isabella* was carried immediately (in her Mourning for her dead Mother) into the Nunnery, and was receiv'd as a very diverting Companion by all the young Ladies, and, above all, by her Reverend Aunt, for she was come just to the Age of delighting her

Parents; she was the prettiest forward Pratler in the World, and had a thousand little Charms to please, besides the young Beauties that were just budding in her little Angel Face: So that she soon became the dear lov'd Favourite of the whole House; and as she was an Entertainment to them all, so they made it their study to find all the Diversions they could for the pretty *Isabella*; and as she grew in Wit and Beauty every day, so they fail'd not to cultivate her Mind; and delicate Apprehension, in all that was advantageous to her Sex, and whatever Excellency any one abounded in, she was sure to communicate it to the young *Isabella*, if one could Dance, another Sing, another play on this Instrument, and another on that; if this spoke one Language, and that another; if she had Wit, and she Discretion, and a third, the finest Fashion and Manners; all joyn'd to compleat the Mind and Body of this beautiful young Girl; Who, being undiverted with the less noble, and less solid, Vanities of the World, took to these Virtues, and excell'd in all; and her Youth and Wit being apt for all Impressions, she soon became a greater Mistress of their Arts, than those who taught her; so that at the Age of eight or nine Years, she was thought fit to receive and entertain all the great Men and Ladies, and the Strangers of any Nation, at the *Grate*; and that with so admirable a Grace, so quick and piercing a Wit, and so delightful and sweet a Conversation, that she became the whole Discourse of the Town, and Strangers spread her Fame, as prodigious, throughout the Christian World; for Strangers came daily to hear her talk, and sing, and play, and to admire her Beauty; and Ladies brought their Children, to shame 'em into good Fashion and Manners, with looking on the lovely young *Isabella*.

The Lady *Abbess*, her Aunt, you may believe, was not a little proud of the Excellencies and Virtues of her fair *Niece*, and omitted nothing that might adorn her Mind; because, not only of the vastness of her Parts and Fame, and the Credit she would do her House, by residing there for ever; but also, being very loth to part with her considerable Fortune, which she must resign, if she returned into the World, she us'd all her Arts and Stratagems to make her become a *Nun*, to which all the fair Sisterhood contributed their Cunning, but it was altogether needless; her Inclination, the strictness of her Devotion, her early Prayers, and those continual, and innate Stedfastness, and Calm, she was Mistress of; her Ignorance of the World's Vanities, and those that uninclos'd young Ladies count Pleasures and Diversions, being all unknown to her, she thought there was no Joy out of a *Nunnery*, and no Satisfactions on the other side of a *Grate*.

The Lady *Abbess*, seeing, that of her self she yielded faster than she could expect; to discharge her Conscience to her Brother, who came frequently to visit his Darling *Isabella*, would very often discourse to her of the Pleasures of the World, telling her, how much happier she would think her self, to be the Wife of some gallant young Cavalier, and to have Coaches and Equipages; to see the World, to behold a thousand Rarities she had never seen, to live in Splendor, to eat high, and wear magnificent Clothes, to be bow'd to as she pass'd, and have a thousand Adorers, to see in time a pretty Offspring, the products of Love, that should talk, and look, and delight, as she did, the Heart of their Parents; but to all, her Father and the Lady *Abbess* could say of the World, and its Pleasures, *Isabella* brought a thousand Reasons and Arguments, so Pious, so Devout, that the *Abbess* was

4

very well pleased, to find her (purposely weak) Propositions so well overthrown; and gives an account of her daily Discourses to her Brother, which were no less pleasing to him; and tho' *Isabella* went already dress'd as richly as her Quality deserv'd, yet her Father, to try the utmost that the World's Vanity could do, upon her young Heart, orders the most Glorious Clothes should be bought her, and that the Lady *Abbess* should suffer her to go abroad with those Ladies of Quality, that were her Relations, and her Mother's Acquaintance; that she should visit and go on the Toore, (that is, the Hide Park there) that she should see all that was diverting, to try, whether it were not for want of Temptation to Vanity, that made her leave the World, and love an inclos'd Life.

As the Count had commanded, all things were performed; and *Isabella* arriving at her Thirteenth Year of Age, and being pretty tall of Stature, with the finest Shape that Fancy can create, with all the Adornment of a perfect brown-hair'd Beauty, Eyes black and lovely, Complexion fair; to a Miracle, all her Features of the rarest proportion, the Mouth red, the Teeth white, and a thousand Graces in her Meen and Air; she came no sooner abroad, but she had a thousand Persons fighting for love of her; the Reputation her Wit had acquir'd, got her Adorers without seeing her, but when they saw her, they found themselves conquer'd and undone; all were glad she was come into the World, of whom they had heard so much, and all the Youth of the Town dress'd only for *Isabella de Valerie*, that rose like a new Star that Eclips'd all the rest, and which set the World a-gazing. Some hop'd, and some despair'd, but all lov'd, while *Isabella* regarded not their Eyes, their distant darling Looks of Love, and their signs of Adoration; she was civil and affable to all, but so reserv'd, that none durst tell her his Passion, or name that strange and abhorr'd thing, *Love*, to her; the Relations with whom she went abroad every day, were fein to force her out, and when she went, 'twas the motive of Civility, and not Satisfaction, that made her go; whatever she saw, she beheld with no admiration, and nothing created wonder in her, tho' never so strange and Novel. She survey'd all things with an indifference, that tho' it was not sullen, was far from Transport, so that her evenness of Mind was infinitely admir'd and prais'd. And now it was, that, young as she was, her Conduct and Discretion appear'd equal to her Wit and Beauty, and she encreas'd daily in Reputation, insomuch, that the Parents of abundance of young Noble Men, made it their business to endeavour to marry their Sons to so admirable and noble a Maid, and one, whose Virtues were the Discourse of all the World; the *Father*, the Lady *Abbess*, and those who had her abroad, were solicited to make an Alliance; for the Father, he would give no answer, but left it to the discretion of *Isabella*, who could not be persuaded to hear any thing of that nature; so that for a long time she refus'd her company to all those, who propos'd any thing of Marriage to her; she said, she had seen nothing in the World that was worth her Care, or the venturing the losing of Heaven for, and therefore was resolv'd to dedicate her self to that; that the more she saw of the World, the worse she lik'd it, and pity'd the Wretches that were condemn'd to it; that she had consider'd it, and found no one Inclination that forbad her immediate Entrance into a Religious Life; to which, her Father, after using all the Arguments he could, to make her take good heed of what she went about, to consider it well; and had urg'd all the Inconveniencies of Severe Life, Watchings, Midnight Risings in all Weathers and Seasons to Prayers, hard Lodging, course Diet, and homely Habit, with a thousand other things of Labour and Work us'd among the *Nuns;* and finding her still resolv'd and inflexible to all contrary persuasions, he consented, kiss'd her, and told her, She had argu'd according to the wish of his Soul, and that he never believ'd himself truly happy, till this moment that he was assur'd, she would become a Religious.

This News, to the Heart-breaking of a thousand Lovers, was spread all over the Town, and there was nothing but Songs of Complaint, and of her retiring, after she had shewn her self to the World, and vanquish'd so many Hearts; all Wits were at work on this Cruel Subject, and one begat another, as is usual in such Affairs. Amongst the number of these Lovers, there was a young Gentleman, Nobly born, his name was *Villenoys,* who was admirably made, and very handsom, had travell'd and accomplish'd himself, as much as was possible for one so young to do; he was about Eighteen, and was going to the Siege of *Candia,* in a very good Equipage, but, overtaken by his Fate, surpris'd in his way to Glory, he stopt at *Ipers,* so fell most passionately in love with this Maid of Immortal Fame; but being defeated in his hopes by this News, was the Man that made the softest Complaints to this fair Beauty, and whose violence of Passion oppress'd him to that degree, that he was the only Lover, who durst himself tell her, he was in love with her; he writ Billets so soft and tender, that she had, of all her Lovers, most compassion for *Villenoys,* and dain'd several times, in pity of him, to send him answers to his Letters, but they were such, as absolutely forbad him to love her; such as incited him to follow Glory, the Mistress that could noblest reward him; and that, for her part, her Prayers should always be, that he might be victorious, and the Darling of that Fortune he was going to court; and that she, for her part, had fix'd her Mind on Heaven, and no Earthly Thought should bring it down; but she should ever retain for him all Sisterly Respect, and begg'd, in her Solitudes, to hear, whether her Prayers had prov'd effectual or not, and if Fortune were so kind to him, as she should perpetually wish.

When *Villenoys* found she was resolv'd, he design'd to persue his Journy, but could not leave the Town, till he had seen the fatal Ceremony of *Isabella's* being made a *Nun,* which was every day expected; and while he stay'd, he could not forbear writing daily to her, but receiv'd no more Answers from her, she already accusing her self of having done too much, for a Maid in her Circumstances; but she confess'd, of all she had seen, she lik'd *Villenoys* the best; and if she ever could have lov'd, she believ'd it would have been *Villenoys,* for he had all the good Qualities, and grace, that could render him agreeable to the Fair; besides, that he was only Son to a very rich and noble Parent, and one that might very well presume to lay claim to a Maid of *Isabella's* Beauty and Fortune.

As the time approach'd, when he must eternally lose all hope, by *Isabella's* taking Orders, he found himself less able to bear the Efforts of that Despair it possess'd him with, he languished with the thought, so that it was visible to all his Friends, the decays it wrought on his Beauty and Gaiety: So that he fell at last into a Feaver; and 'twas the whole Discourse of the Town, That *Villenoys* was dying for the Fair *Isabella;* his Relations, being all of Quality, were extreamly afflicted at his Misfortune, and joyn'd their Interests yet, to dissuade this fair young Victoress from an act so cruel, as to inclose herself in a *Nunnery*, while the finest of all the youths of Quality was dying for her, and ask'd her, If it would not be more acceptable to Heaven to save a Life, and perhaps a Soul, than to go and expose her own to a thousand Tortures? They assur'd her, *Villenoys* was dying, and dying Adoring her; that nothing could save his Life, but her kind Eyes turn'd upon the fainting Lover; a Lover, that could breath nothing, but her Name in Sighs; and find satisfaction in nothing, but weeping and crying out, 'I dye for Isabella!' This Discourse fetch'd abundance of Tears from the fair Eyes of this tender Maid; but, at the same time, she besought them to believe, these Tears ought not to give them hope, she should ever yield to save his Life, by quitting her Resolution, of becoming a *Nun*; but, on the contrary, they were Tears, that only bewail'd her own Misfortune, in having been the occasion of the death of any Man, especially, a Man, who had so many Excellencies, as might have render'd him entirely Happy and Glorious for a long race of Years, had it not been his ill fortune to have seen her unlucky Face. She believ'd, it was for her Sins of Curiosity, and going beyond the Walls of the Monastery, to wander after the Vanities of the foolish World, that had occasion'd this Misfortune to the young Count of *Villenoys*, and she would put a severe Penance on her Body, for the Mischiefs her Eyes had done him; she fears she might, by something in her looks, have intic'd his Heart, for she own'd she saw him, with wonder at his Beauty, and much more she admir'd him, when she found the Beauties of his Mind; she confess'd, she had given him hope, by answering his Letters; and that when she found her Heart grow a little more than usually tender, when she thought on him, she believ'd it a Crime, that ought to be check'd by a Virtue, such as she pretended to profess, and hop'd she should ever carry to her Grave; and she desired his Relations to implore him, in her Name, to rest contented, in knowing he was the first, and should be the last, that should ever make an impression on her Heart; that what she had conceiv'd there, for him, should remain with her to her dying day, and that she besought him to live, that she might see, he both deserv'd this Esteem she had for him, and to repay it her, otherwise he would dye in her debt, and make her Life ever after reposeless.

This being all they could get from her, they return'd with Looks that told their Message; however, they render'd those soft things *Isabella* had said, in so moving a manner, as fail'd not to please, and while he remain'd in this condition, the Ceremonies were compleated, of making *Isabella* a *Nun*, which was a Secret to none but *Villenoys*, and from him it was carefully conceal'd, so that in a little time he recover'd his lost health, at least, so well, as to support the fatal News, and upon the first hearing it, he made ready his Equipage, and departed immediately for *Candia*; where he behav'd himself very gallantly, under the Command of the Duke De *Beaufort*, and, with him, return'd to *France*, after the loss of that noble City to the *Turks*.

In all the time of his absence, that he might the sooner establish his Repose, he forbore sending to the fair Cruel *Nun*, and she heard no more of *Villenoys* in above two years; so that giving her self wholly up to Devotion, there was never seen any one, who led so

7

She thinks she's done something wrong because she likes him. → "She feard" she looked good & enticed him.

Austere and Pious a Life, as this young *Votress*; she was a Saint in the Chapel, and an Angel at the *Grate*: She there laid by all her severe Looks, and mortify'd Discourse, and being at perfect peace and tranquility within, she was outwardly all gay, sprightly, and entertaining, being satisfy'd, no Sights, no Freedoms, could give any temptations to worldly desires; she gave a loose to all that was modest, and that Virtue and Honour would permit, and was the most charming Conversation that ever was admir'd; and the whole World that pass'd through *Iper*, of Strangers, came directed and recommended to the lovely *Isabella*; I mean, those of Quality: But however Diverting she was at the *Grate*, she was most exemplary Devout in the Cloister, doing more Penance, and imposing a more rigid Severity and Task on her self, than was requir'd, giving such rare Examples to all the *Nuns* that were less Devout, that her Life was a Proverb, and a President, and when they would express a very Holy Woman indeed, they would say, 'She was a very *ISABELLA*.'

There was in this *Nunnery*, a young *Nun*, call'd, Sister *Katteriena*, Daughter to the Grave *Vanhenault*, that is to say, an Earl, who liv'd about six Miles from the Town, in a noble *Villa*; this Sister *Katteriena* was not only a very beautiful Maid, but very witty, and had all the good qualities to make her be belov'd, and had most wonderfully gain'd upon the Heart of the fair *Isabella*, she was her Chamber–Fellow and Companion in all her Devotions and Diversions, so that where one was, there was the other, and they never went but together to the *Grate*, to the Garden, or to any place, whither their *Affairs* call'd either. This young *Katteriena* had a Brother, who lov'd her intirely, and came every day to see her, he was about twenty Years of Age, rather tall than middle Statur'd, his Hair and Eyes brown, but his Face exceeding beautiful, adorn'd with a thousand Graces, and the most nobly and exactly made, that 'twas possible for Nature to form; to the Fineness and Charms of his Person, he had an Air in his Meen and Dressing, so very agreeable, besides rich, that 'twas impossible to look on him, without wishing him happy, because he did so absolutely merit being so. His Wit and his Manner was so perfectly Obliging, a Goodness and Generosity so Sincere and Gallant, that it would even have aton'd for Ugliness. As he was eldest Son to so great a Father, he was kept at home, while the rest of his Brothers were employ'd in Wars abroad; this made him of a melancholy Temper, and fit for soft Impressions; he was very Bookish, and had the best Tutors that could be got, for Learning and Languages, and all that could compleat a Man; but was unus'd to Action, and of a temper Lazy, and given to Repose, so that his Father could hardly ever get him to use any Exercise, or so much as ride abroad, which he would call, Losing Time from his Studies: He car'd not for the Conversation of Men, because he lov'd not Debauch, as they usually did; so that for Exercise, more than any Design, he came on Horseback every day to *Iper* to the *Monastery*, and would sit at the *Grate*, entertaining his Sister the most part of the Afternoon, and, in the Evening, retire; he had often seen and convers'd with the lovely *Isabella*, and found from the first sight of her, he had more Esteem for her, than any other of her Sex: But as Love very rarely takes Birth without Hope; so he never believ'd that the Pleasure he took in beholding her, and in discoursing with her, was Love, because he regarded her, as a Thing consecrate to Heaven, and never so much as thought to wish, she were a Mortal fit for his Addresses; yet he found himself more and more fill'd with Reflections on her which was not usual with him; he found she grew upon his Memory, and oftner came there, than he us'd to do, that he lov'd his Studies less, and going to *Iper* more; and, that every time he went, he found a new Joy at his Heart that pleas'd him; he found, he could not get himself from the *Grate*, without Pain; nor part from the sight of that all–charming Object, without Sighs; and if, while he was there, any persons came to visit her, whose Quality she could not refuse the honour of her sight to, he would blush, and pant with uneasiness, especially, if they were handsom, and fit to make Impressions: And he would check this Uneasiness in himself, and ask his Heart, what it meant, by rising and beating in those Moments, and strive to assume an Indifferency in vain, and depart dissatisfy'd, and out of humour.

On the other side, *Isabella* was not so Gay as she us'd to be, but, on the sudden, retir'd her self more from the *Grate* than she us'd to do, refus'd to receive Visits every day, and her Complexion grew a little pale and languid; she was observ'd not to sleep, or eat, as she us'd to do, nor exercise in those little Plays they made, and diverted themselves with, now and then; she was heard to sigh often, and it became the Discourse of the whole House, that she was much alter'd: The Lady *Abbess*, who lov'd her with a most tender Passion, was infinitely concern'd at this Change, and endeavour'd to find out the Cause, and 'twas generally believ'd, she was too Devout, for now she redoubled her Austerity; and in cold Winter Nights, of Frost and Snow, would be up at all Hours, and lying upon the cold Stones, before the Altar, prostrate at Prayers: So that she receiv'd Orders from the Lady *Abbess*, not to harass her self so very much, but to have a care of her Health, as well as her Soul; but she regarded not these Admonitions, tho' even persuaded daily by her *Katteriena*, whom she lov'd every day more and more.

But, one Night, when they were retir'd to their Chamber, amongst a thousand things that they spoke of, to pass away a tedious Evening, they talk'd of Pictures and Likenesses, and *Katteriena* told *Isabella*, that before she was a *Nun*, in her more happy days, she was so like her Brother *Bernardo Henault*, (who was the same that visited them every day) that she would, in Men's Clothes, undertake, she should not have known one from t'other, and fetching out his *Picture*, she had in a Dressing–Box, she threw it to *Isabella*, who, at the first sight of it, turns as pale as Ashes, and, being ready to swound, she bid her take it away, and could not, for her Soul, hide the sudden surprise the *Picture* brought: *Katteriena* had too much Wit, not to make a just Interpretation of this Change, and (as a Woman) was naturally curious to pry farther, tho' Discretion should have made her been silent, for Talking, in such cases, does but make the Wound rage the more; 'Why, my dear Sister, (said *Katteriena*) is the likeness of my Brother so offensive to you?' *Isabella* found by this, she had discover'd too much, and that Thought put her by all power of excusing it; she was confounded with Shame, and the more she strove to hide it, the more it disorder'd her; so that she (blushing extremely) hung down her Head, sigh'd, and confess'd all by her Looks. At last, after a considering Pause, she cry'd, 'My dearest Sister, I do confess, I was surpriz'd at the sight of Monsieur *Henault*, and much more than ever you have observ'd

She would dress as a man?

9

me to be at the sight of his Person, because there is scarce a day wherein I do not see that, and know beforehand I shall see him; I am prepar'd for the Encounter, and have lessen'd my Concern, or rather Confusion, by that time I come to the *Grate*, so much Mistress I am of my Passions, when they give me warning of their approach, and sure I can withstand the greatest assaults of Fate, if I can but foresee it; but if it surprize me, I find I am as feeble a Woman, as the most unresolv'd; you did not tell me, you had this Picture, nor say, you would shew me such a Picture; but when I least expect to see that Face, you shew it me, even in my Chamber.'

'Ah, my dear Sister! (reply'd *Katteriena*) I believe, that Paleness, and those Blushes, proceed from some other cause, than the Nicety of seeing the Picture of a Man in your Chamber':

'You have too much Wit, (reply'd *Isabella*) to be impos'd on by such an Excuse, if I were so silly to make it; but oh! my dear Sister! it was in my Thoughts to deceive you; could I have concealed my Pain and Sufferings, you should never have known them; but since I find it impossible, and that I am too sincere to make use of Fraud in any thing, 'tis fit I tell you, from what cause my change of Colour proceeds, and to own to you, I fear, 'tis Love, if ever therefore, oh gentle pitying Maid! thou wert a Lover? If ever thy tender Heart were touch'd with that Passion? Inform me, oh! inform me, of the nature of that cruel Disease, and how thou found'st a Cure?'

While she was speaking these words, she threw her Arms about the Neck of the fair *Katteriena*, and bath'd her Bosom (where she hid her Face) with a shower of Tears; *Katteriena*, embracing her with all the fondness of a dear Lover, told her, with a Sigh, that she could deny her nothing, and therefore confess'd to her, she had been a Lover, and that was the occasion of her being made a *Nun*, her Father finding out the Intrigue, which fatally happened to be with his own Page, a Youth of extraordinary Beauty. 'I was but Young, (said she) about Thirteen, and knew not what to call the new-known Pleasure that I felt; when e're I look'd upon the young *Arnaldo*, my Heart would heave, when e're he came in view, and my disorder'd Breath came doubly from my Bosom; a Shivering seiz'd me, and my Face grew wan; my Thought was at a stand, and Sense it self, for that short moment, lost its Faculties; But when he touch'd me, oh! no hunted Deer, tir'd with his flight, and just secur'd in Shades, pants with a nimbler motion than my Heart; at first, I thought the Youth had had some Magick Art, to make one faint and tremble at his touches; but he himself, when I accus'd his Cruelty, told me, he had no Art, but awful Passion, and vow'd that when I touch'd him, he was so; so trembling, so surprized, so charm'd, so pleas'd. When he was present, nothing could displease me, but when he parted from me; then 'twas rather a soft silent Grief, that eas'd itself by sighing, and by hoping, that some kind moment would restore my joy. When he was absent, nothing could divert me, howe're I strove, howe're I toyl'd for Mirth; no Smile, no Joy, dwelt in my Heart or Eyes; I could not feign, so very well I lov'd, impatient in his absence, I would count the tedious parting Hours, and pass them off like useless Visitants, whom we wish were gon; these are the

Hours, where Life no business has, at least, a Lover's Life. But, oh! what Minutes seem'd the happy Hours, when on his Eyes I gaz'd, and he on mine, and half our Conversation lost in Sighs, Sighs, the soft moving Language of a Lover!'

'No more, no more, (reply'd *Isabella*, throwing her Arms again about the Neck of the transported *Katteriena*) thou blow'st my Flame by thy soft Words, and mak'st me know my Weakness, and my Shame: I love! I love! and feel those differing Passions!'—Then pausing a moment, she proceeded,—'Yet so didst thou, but hast surmounted it. Now thou hast found the Nature of my Pain, oh! tell me thy saving Remedy?' 'Alas! (reply'd *Katteriena*) tho' there's but one Disease, there's many Remedies: They say, possession's one, but that to me seems a Riddle; Absence, they say, another, and that was mine; for *Arnaldo* having by chance lost one of my Billets, discover'd the Amour, and was sent to travel, and my self forc'd into this Monastery, where at last, Time convinc'd me, I had lov'd below my Quality, and that sham'd me into Holy Orders.' 'And is it a Disease, (reply'd *Isabella*) that People often recover?' 'Most frequently, (said *Katteriena*) and yet some dye of the Disease, but very rarely.' 'Nay then, (said *Isabella*) I fear, you will find me one of these Martyrs; for I have already oppos'd it with the most severe Devotion in the World: But all my Prayers are vain, your lovely Brother persues me into the greatest Solitude; he meets me at my very Midnight Devotions, and interrupts my Prayers; he gives me a thousand Thoughts, that ought not to enter into a Soul dedicated to Heaven; he ruins all the Glory I have achiev'd, even above my Sex, for Piety of Life, and the Observation of all Virtues. Oh *Katteriena!* he has a Power in his Eyes, that transcends all the World besides: And, to shew the weakness of Human Nature, and how vain all our Boastings are, he has done that in one fatal Hour, that the persuasions of all my Relations and Friends, Glory, Honour, Pleasure, and all that can tempt, could not perform in Years; I resisted all but *Henault's* Eyes, and they were Ordain'd to make me truly wretched; But yet with thy Assistance, and a Resolution to see him no more, and my perpetual Trust in Heaven, I may, perhaps, overcome this Tyrant of my Soul, who, I thought, had never enter'd into holy Houses, or mix'd his Devotions and Worship with the true Religion; but, oh! no Cells, no Cloysters, no Hermitages, are secur'd from his Efforts.'

This Discourse she ended with abundance of Tears, and it was resolv'd, since she was devoted for ever to a Holy Life, That it was best for her to make it as easy to her as was possible; in order to it, and the banishing this fond and useless Passion from her Heart, it was very necessary, she should see *Henault* no more: At first, *Isabella* was afraid, that, in refusing to see him, he might mistrust her Passion; but *Katteriena* who was both Pious and Discreet, and endeavour'd truly to cure her of so violent a Disease, which must, she knew, either end in her death or destruction, told her, She would take care of that matter, that it should not blemish her Honour; and so leaving her a while, after they had resolved on this, she left her in a thousand Confusions, she was now another Woman than what she had hitherto been; she was quite alter'd in every Sentiment, thought and Notion; she now repented, she had promis'd not to see *Henault*; she trembled and even fainted, for fear she should see him no more; she was not able to bear that thought, it made her rage within,

11

like one possest, and all her Virtue could not calm her; yet since her word was past, and, as she was, she could not, without great Scandal, break it in that point, she resolv'd to dye a thousand Deaths, rather than not perform her Promise made to *Katteriena*; but 'tis not to be express'd what she endur'd; what Fits, Pains, and Convulsions, she sustain'd; and how much ado she had to dissemble to Dame *Katteriena*, who soon return'd to the afflicted Maid; the next day, about the time that *Henault* was to come, as he usually did, about two or three a Clock after Noon, 'tis impossible to express the uneasiness of *Isabella*; she ask'd, a thousand times, 'What, is not your Brother come?' When Dame *Katteriena* would reply, 'Why do you ask?' She would say, 'Because I would be sure not to see him': 'You need not fear, Madam, (reply'd *Katteriena*) for you shall keep your Chamber.' She need not have urg'd that, for *Isabella* was very ill without knowing it, and in a Feaver.

At last, one of the *Nuns* came up, and told Dame *Katteriena*, that her Brother was at the *Grate*, and she desired, he should be bid come about to the Private *Grate* above stairs, which he did, and she went to him, leaving *Isabella* even dead on the Bed, at the very name of *Henault*. But the more she conceal'd her Flame, the more violently it rag'd, which she strove in vain by Prayers, and those Recourses of Solitude to lessen; all this did but augment the Pain, and was Oyl to the Fire, so that she now could hope, that nothing but Death would put an end to her Griefs, and her Infamy. She was eternally thinking on him, how handsome his Face, how delicate every Feature, how charming his Air, how graceful his Meen, how soft and good his Disposition, and how witty and entertaining his Conversation. She now fancy'd, she was at the *Grate*, talking to him as she us'd to be, and blest those happy Hours she past then, and bewail'd her Misfortune, that she is no more destin'd to be so Happy, then gives a loose to Grief; Griefs, at which, no Mortals, but Despairing Lovers, can guess, or how tormenting they are; where the most easie Moments are, those, wherein one resolves to kill ones self, and the happiest Thought is Damnation; but from these Imaginations, she endeavours to fly, all frighted with horror; but, alas! whither would she fly, but to a Life more full of horror? She considers well, she cannot bear Despairing Love, and finds it impossible to cure her Despair; she cannot fly from the Thoughts of the Charming *Henault*, and 'tis impossible to quit 'em; and, at this rate, she found, Life could not long support it self, but would either reduce her to Madness, and so render her an hated Object of Scorn to the Censuring World, or force her Hand to commit a Murder upon her self. This she had found, this she had well consider'd, nor could her fervent and continual Prayers, her nightly Watchings, her Mortifications on the cold Marble in long Winter Season, and all her Acts of Devotion abate one spark of this shameful Feaver of Love, that was destroying her within. When she had rag'd and struggled with this unruly Passion, 'till she was quite tir'd and breathless, finding all her force in vain, she fill'd her fancy with a thousand charming *Ideas* of the lovely *Henault*, and, in that soft fit, had a mind to satisfy her panting Heart, and give it one Joy more, by beholding the Lord of its Desires, and the Author of its Pains: Pleas'd, yet trembling, at this Resolve, she rose from the Bed where she was laid, and softly advanc'd to the Stair-Case, from whence there open'd that Room where Dame *Katteriena* was, and where there was a private *Grate*, at which, she was entertaining her *Brother*; they were earnest in Discourse, and so loud, that *Isabella* could easily hear all they said, and the first words were from *Katteriena*, who, in a sort of Anger, cry'd, 'Urge me no more! My Virtue is too nice, to become an Advocate for a Passion, that can tend to nothing but your Ruin; for, suppose I should tell the fair *Isabella*, you dye for her, what can it avail you? What hope can any Man have, to move the Heart of a Virgin, so averse to Love? A Virgin, whose Modesty and Virtue is so very curious, it would fly the very word, Love, as some monstrous Witchcraft, or the foulest of Sins, who would loath me for bringing so lewd a Message, and banish you her Sight, as the Object of her Hate and Scorn; is it unknown to you, how many of the noblest Youths of *Flanders* have address'd themselves to her in vain, when yet she was in the World? Have you been ignorant, how the young Count de *Villenoys* languished, in vain, almost to Death for her? And, that no Persuasions, no Attractions in him, no wordly Advantages, or all his Pleadings, who had a Wit and Spirit capable of prevailing on any Heart, less severe and harsh, than hers? Do you not know, that all was lost on this insensible fair one, even when she was a proper Object for the Adoration of the Young and Amorous? And can you hope, now she has so entirely wedded her future days to Devotion, and given all to Heaven; nay, lives a Life here more like a Saint, than a Woman; rather an Angel, than a mortal Creature? Do you imagin, with any Rhetorick you can deliver, now to turn the Heart, and whole Nature, of this Divine Maid, to consider your Earthly Passion? No, 'tis fondness, and an injury to her Virtue, to harbour such a Thought; quit it, quit it, my dear Brother! before it ruin your Repose.' 'Ah, Sister! (replied the dejected *Henault*) your Counsel comes too late, and your Reasons are of too feeble force, to rebate those Arrows, the Charming *Isabella's* Eyes have fix'd in my Heart and Soul; and I am undone, unless she know my Pain, which I shall dye, before I shall ever dare mention to her; but you, young Maids, have a thousand Familiarities together, can jest, and play, and say a thousand things between Railery and Earnest, that may first hint what you would deliver, and insinuate into each others Hearts a kind of Curiosity to know more; for naturally, (my dear Sister) Maids, are curious and vain; and however Divine the Mind of the fair *Isabella* may be, it bears the Tincture still of Mortal Woman.'

'Suppose this true, how could this Mortal part about her Advantage you, (said *Katteriena*) all that you can expect from this Discovery, (if she should be content to hear it, and to return you pity) would be, to make her wretched, like your self? What farther can you hope?' 'Oh! talk not, (replied *Henault*) of so much Happiness! I do not expect to be so blest, that she should pity me, or love to a degree of Inquietude; 'tis sufficient, for the ease of my Heart, that she know its Pains, and what it suffers for her; that she would give my Eyes leave to gaze upon her, and my Heart to vent a Sigh now and then; and, when I dare, to give me leave to speak, and tell her of my Passion; This, this, is all, my Sister.' And, at that word, the Tears glided down his Cheeks, and he declin'd his Eyes, and set a Look so charming, and so sad, that *Isabella*, whose Eyes were fix'd upon him, was a thousand times ready to throw her self into the Room, and to have made a Confession, how sensible she was of all she had heard and seen: But, with much ado, she contain'd and satisfy'd her self, with knowing, that she was ador'd by him whom she ador'd, and, with Prudence that is natural to her, she withdrew, and waited with patience the event of their Discourse. She impatiently long'd to know, how *Katteriena* would manage this Secret her Brother had given her, and was pleas'd, that the Friendship and Prudence of that Maid had conceal'd her Passion from her Brother; and now contented and joyful beyond imagination, to find her self belov'd, she knew she could dissemble her own Passion and make him the first Aggressor; the first that lov'd, or at least, that should seem to do so. This Thought restores her so great a part of her Peace of Mind, that she resolv'd to see him, and to dissemble with *Katteriena* so far, as to make her believe, she had subdu'd that Passion, she was really asham'd to own; she now, with her Woman's Skill, begins to practise an Art she never before understood, and has recourse to Cunning, and resolves to seem to reassume her former Repose: But hearing *Katteriena* approach, she laid her self again on her Bed, where she had left her, but compos'd her Face to more chearfulness, and put on a Resolution that indeed deceiv'd the Sister, who was extreamly pleased, she said, to see her look so well: When *Isabella* reply'd, 'Yes, I am another Woman now; I hope Heaven has heard, and granted, my long and humble Supplications, and driven from my Heart this tormenting God, that has so long disturb'd my purer Thoughts.' 'And are you sure, (said Dame *Katteriena*) that this wanton Deity is repell'd by the noble force of your Resolutions? Is he never to return?' 'No, (replied *Isabella*) never to my Heart.' 'Yes, (said *Katteriena*) if you should see the lovely Murderer of your Repose, your Wound would bleed anew.' At this, *Isabella* smiling with a little Disdain, reply'd, 'Because you once to love, and *Henault's* Charms defenceless found me, ah! do you think I have no Fortitude? But so in Fondness lost, remiss in Virtue, that when I have resolv'd, (and see it necessary for my after-Quiet) to want the power of keeping that Resolution? No, scorn me, and despise me then, as lost to all the Glories of my Sex, and all that Nicety I've hitherto preserv'd.' There needed no more from a Maid of *Isabella's* Integrity and Reputation, to convince any one of the Sincerity of what she said, since, in the whole course of her Life, she never could be charg'd with an Untruth, or an Equivocation; and *Katteriena* assur'd her, she believ'd her, and was infinitely glad she had vanquish'd a Passion, that would have prov'd destructive to her Repose: *Isabella* reply'd, She had not altogether vanquish'd her Passion, she did not boast of so absolute a power over her soft Nature, but had resolv'd things great, and Time would work the Cure; that she hop'd, *Katteriena* would make such Excuses to her Brother, for her not appearing at the *Grate* so gay and entertaining as she us'd, and, by a little absence, she should retrieve the Liberty she had lost: But she desir'd, such Excuses might be made for her, that young *Henault* might not perceive the Reason. At the naming him, she had much ado not to shew some Concern extraordinary, and *Katteriena* assur'd her, She had now a very good Excuse to keep from the *Grate*, when he was at it; 'For, (said she) now you have resolv'd, I may tell you, he is dying for you, raving in Love, and has this day made me promise to him, to give you some account of his Passion, and to make you sensible of his Languishment: I had not told you this, (reply'd *Katteriena*) but that I believe you fortify'd with brave Resolution and Virtue, and that this knowledge will rather put you more upon your Guard, than you were before.' While she spoke, she fixed her Eyes on *Isabella*, to see what alteration it would make in her Heart and Looks; but the Master-piece of this young Maid's Art was shewn in this minute, for she commanded her self so well, that her very Looks dissembled and shew'd no concern at a Relation, that made her Soul dance with Joy; but it was, what she was prepar'd for, or else I question her Fortitude. But, with a Calmness, which absolutely subdu'd *Katteriena*, she reply'd, 'I am almost glad he has confess'd a Passion for me, and you shall confess to him, you told me of it, and that I absent my self from the *Grate*, on purpose to avoid the sight of a Man, who durst love me, and confess it; and I assure you, my dear Sister! (continued she, dissembling) You could not have advanc'd my Cure by a more effectual way, than telling me of his Presumption.' At that word, *Katteriena* joyfully related to her all that had pass'd between young *Henault* and her self, and how he implor'd her Aid in this Amour; at the end of which Relation, *Isabella* smil'd, and carelesly reply'd, 'I pity him': And so going to their Devotion, they had no more Discourse of the Lover.

In the mean time, young *Henault* was a little satisfy'd, to know, his Sister would discover his Passion to the lovely *Isabella*; and though he dreaded the return, he was pleas'd that she should know, she had a Lover that ador'd her, though even without hope; for though the thought of possessing *Isabella*, was the most ravishing that could be; yet he had a dread upon him, when he thought of it, for he could not hope to accomplish that, without Sacrilege; and he was a young Man, very Devout, and even bigotted in Religion; and would often question and debate within himself, that, if it were possible, he should come to be belov'd by this Fair Creature, and that it were possible for her, to grant all that Youth in Love could require, whether he should receive the Blessing offer'd? And though he ador'd the Maid, whether he should not abhor the *Nun* in his Embraces? 'Twas an undetermin'd Thought, that chill'd his Fire as often as it approach'd; but he had too many that rekindled it again with the greater Flame and Ardor.

His impatience to know, what Success *Katteriena* had, with the Relation she was to make to *Isabella* in his behalf, brought him early to *Iper* the next day. He came again to the private *Grate*, where his Sister receiving him, and finding him, with a sad and dejected Look, expect what she had to say; she told him, That Look well became the News she had for him, it being such, as ought to make him, both Griev'd, and Penitent; for, to obey him, she had so absolutely displeas'd *Isabella*, that she was resolv'd never to believe her her Friend more, 'Or to see you, (said she) therefore, as you have made me commit a Crime against my Conscience, against my Order, against my Friendship, and against my Honour, you ought to do some brave thing; take some noble Resolution, worthy of your Courage, to redeem all; for your Repose, I promis'd, I would let Isabella know you lov'd, and, for the mitigation of my Crime, you ought to let me tell her, you have surmounted your Passion, as the last Remedy of Life and Fame.'

At these her last words, the Tears gush'd from his Eyes, and he was able only, a good while, to sigh; at last, cry'd, 'What! see her no more! see the Charming *Isabella* no more!' And then vented the Grief of his Soul in so passionate a manner, as his Sister had all the Compassion imaginable for him, but thought it great Sin and Indiscretion to cherish his Flame: So that, after a while, having heard her Counsel, he reply'd, 'And is this all, my

15

Sister, you will do to save a Brother?' 'All! (reply'd she) I would not be the occasion of making a *NUN* violate her Vow, to save a Brother's Life, no, nor my own; assure your self of this, and take it as my last Resolution: Therefore, if you will be content with the Friendship of this young Lady, and so behave your self, that we may find no longer the Lover in the Friend, we shall reassume our former Conversation, and live with you, as we ought; otherwise, your Presence will continually banish her from the *Grate*, and, in time, make both her you love, and your self, a Town Discourse.'

Much more to this purpose she said, to dissuade him, and bid him retire, and keep himself from thence, till he could resolve to visit them without a Crime; and she protested, if he did not do this, and master his foolish Passion, she would let her Father understand his Conduct, who was a Man of temper so very precise, that should he believe, his Son should have a thought of Love to a Virgin vow'd to Heaven, he would abandon him to Shame, and eternal Poverty, by disinheriting him of all he could: Therefore, she said, he ought to lay all this to his Heart, and weigh it with his unheedy Passion. While the Sister talk'd thus wisely, *Henault* was not without his Thoughts, but consider'd as she spoke, but did not consider in the right place; he was not considering, how to please a Father, and save an Estate, but how to manage the matter so, to establish himself, as he was before with *Isabella*; for he imagin'd, since already she knew his Passion, and that if after that she would be prevail'd with to see him, he might, some lucky Minute or other, have the pleasure of speaking for himself, at least, he should again see and talk to her, which was a joyful Thought in the midst of so many dreadful ones: And, as if he had known what pass'd in *Isabella's* Heart, he, by a strange sympathy, took the same measures to deceive *Katteriena*, a well-meaning young Lady, and easily impos'd on from her own Innocence, he resolv'd to dissemble Patience, since he must have that Virtue, and own'd, his Sister's Reasons were just, and ought to be persu'd; that she had argu'd him into half his Peace, and that he would endeavour to recover the rest; that Youth ought to be pardon'd a thousand Failings, and Years would reduce him to a condition of laughing at his Follies of Youth, but that grave Direction was not yet arriv'd: And so desiring, she would pray for his Conversion, and that she would recommend him to the Devotions of the Fair *Isabella*, he took his leave, and came no more to the *Nunnery* in ten Days; in all which time, none but Impatient Lovers can guess, what Pain and Languishments *Isabella* suffer'd, not knowing the Cause of his Absence, nor daring to enquire; but she bore it out so admirably, that Dame *Katteriena* never so much as suspected she had any Thoughts of that nature that perplex'd her, and now believ'd indeed she had conquer'd all her Uneasiness: And one day, when *Isabella* and she were alone together, she ask'd that fair Dissembler, if she did not admire at the Conduct and Resolution of her Brother? 'Why!' (reply'd *Isabella* unconcernedly, while her Heart was fainting within, for fear of ill News:) With that, *Katteriena* told her the last Discourse she had with her Brother, and how at last she had persuaded him (for her sake) to quit his Passion; and that he had promis'd, he would endeavour to surmount it; and that, that was the reason he was absent now, and they were to see him no more, till he had made a Conquest over himself. You may assure your self, this News was not so welcom to *Isabella*, as *Katteriena* imagin'd; yet still she dissembled, with a force, beyond what the

16

most cunning Practitioner could have shewn, and carry'd her self before People, as if no Pressures had lain upon her Heart; but when alone retir'd, in order to her Devotion, she would vent her Griefs in the most deplorable manner, that a distress'd distracted Maid could do, and which, in spite of all her severe Penances, she found no abatement of.

At last *Henault* came again to the *Monastery*, and, with a Look as gay as he could possibly assume, he saw his Sister, and told her, He had gain'd an absolute Victory over his Heart; and desir'd, he might see *Isabella*, only to convince, both her, and *Katteriena*, that he was no longer a Lover of that fair Creature, that had so lately charm'd him; that he had set Five thousand Pounds a Year, against a fruitless Passion, and found the solid Gold much the heavier in the Scale: And he smil'd, and talk'd the whole Day of indifferent things, with his Sister, and ask'd no more for *Isabella*; nor did *Isabella* look, or ask, after him, but in her Heart. Two Months pass'd in this Indifference, till it was taken notice of, that Sister *Isabella* came not to the *Grate*, when *Henault* was there, as she us'd to do; this being spoken to Dame *Katteriena*, she told it to *Isabella*, and said, 'The *NUNS* would believe, there was some Cause for her Absence, if she did not appear again': That if she could trust her Heart, she was sure she could trust her Brother, for he thought no more of her, she was confident; this, in lieu of pleasing, was a Dagger to the Heart of *Isabella*, who thought it time to retrieve the flying Lover, and therefore told *Katteriena*, She would the next Day entertain at the Low *Grate*, as she was wont to do, and accordingly, as soon as any People of Quality came, she appear'd there, where she had not been two Minutes, but she saw the lovely *Henault*, and it was well for both, that People were in the Room, they had else both sufficiently discover'd their Inclinations, or rather their not to be conceal'd Passions; after the General Conversation was over, by the going away of the Gentlemen that were at the *Grate*, *Katteriena* being employ'd elsewhere, *Isabella* was at last left alone with *Henault*; but who can guess the Confusion of these two Lovers, who wish'd, yet fear'd, to know each others Thoughts? She trembling with a dismal Apprehension, that he lov'd no more; and he almost dying with fear, she should Reproach or Upbraid him with his Presumption; so that both being possess'd with equal Sentiments of Love, Fear, and Shame, they both stood fix'd with dejected Looks and Hearts, that heav'd with stifled Sighs. At last, *Isabella*, the softer and tender-hearted of the two, tho' not the most a Lover perhaps, not being able to contain her Love any longer within the bounds of Dissimulation or Discretion, being by Nature innocent, burst out into Tears, and all fainting with pressing Thoughts within, she fell languishly into a Chair that stood there, while the distracted *Henault*, who could not come to her Assistance, and finding Marks of Love, rather than Anger or Disdain, in that Confusion of *Isabella's*, throwing himself on his Knees at the *Grate*, implor'd her to behold him, to hear him, and to pardon him, who dy'd every moment for her, and who ador'd her with a violent Ardor; but yet, with such an one, as should (tho' he perish'd with it) be conformable to her Commands; and as he spoke, the Tears stream'd down his dying Eyes, that beheld her with all the tender Regard that ever Lover was capable of; she recover'd a little, and turn'd her too beautiful Face to him, and pierc'd him with a Look, that darted a thousand Joys and Flames into his Heart, with Eyes, that told him her Heart was burning and dying for him; for which Assurances, he made Ten

17

thousand Asseverations of his never-dying Passion, and expressing as many Raptures and Excesses of Joy, to find her Eyes and Looks confess, he was not odious to her, and that the knowledge he was her Lover, did not make her hate him: In fine, he spoke so many things all soft and moving, and so well convinc'd her of his Passion, that she at last was compell'd by a mighty force, absolutely irresistible, to speak.

'Sir, (said she) perhaps you will wonder, where I, a Maid, brought up in the simplicity of Virtue, should learn the Confidence, not only to hear of Love from you, but to confess I am sensible of the most violent of its Pain my self: and I wonder, and am amazed at my own Daring, that I should have the Courage, rather to speak, than dye, and bury it in silence; but such is my Fate. Hurried by an unknown Force, which I have endeavoured always, in vain, to resist, I am compell'd to tell you, I love you, and have done so from the first moment I saw you; and you are the only Man born to give me Life or Death, to make me Happy or Blest; perhaps, had I not been confin'd, and, as it were, utterly forbid by my Vow, as well as my Modesty, to tell you this, I should not have been so miserable to have fallen thus low, as to have confess'd my Shame; but our Opportunities of Speaking are so few, and Letters so impossible to be sent without discovery, that perhaps this is the only time I shall ever have to speak with you alone.' And, at that word the Tears flow'd abundantly from her Eyes, and gave *Henault* leave to speak. 'Ah Madam! (said he) do not, as soon as you have rais'd me to the greatest Happiness in the World, throw me with one word beneath your Scorn, much easier 'tis to dye, and know I am lov'd, than never, never, hope to hear that blessed sound again from that beautiful Mouth: Ah, Madam! rather let me make use of this one opportunity our happy Luck has given us, and contrive how we may for ever see, and speak, to each other; let us assure one another, there are a thousand ways to escape a place so rigid, as denies us that Happiness; and denies the fairest Maid in the World, the privilege of her Creation, and the end to which she was form'd so Angelical.' And seeing *Isabella* was going to speak, lest she should say something, that might dissuade from an Attempt so dangerous and wicked, he persu'd to tell her, it might be indeed the last moment Heaven would give 'em, and besought her to answer him what he implor'd, whether she would fly with him from the *Monastery*? At this Word, she grew pale, and started, as at some dreadful Sound, and cry'd, 'Hah! what is't you say? Is it possible, you should propose a thing so wicked? And can it enter into your Imagination, because I have so far forget my Virtue, and my Vow, to become a Lover, I should therefore fall to so wretched a degree of Infamy and Reprobation? No, name it to me no more, if you would see me; and if it be as you say, a Pleasure to be belov'd by me; for I will sooner dye, than yield to what . . . Alas! I but too well approve!' These last words, she spoke with a fainting Tone, and the Tears fell anew from her fair soft Eyes. 'If it be so,' said he, (with a Voice so languishing, it could scarce be heard) 'If it be so, and that you are resolv'd to try, if my Love be eternal without Hope, without expectation of any other Joy, than seeing and adoring you through the *Grate*; I am, and must, and will be contented, and you shall see, I can prefer the Sighing to these cold Irons, that separate us, before all the Possessions of the rest of the World; that I chuse rather to lead my Life here, at this cruel Distance from you, for ever, than before the Embrace of all the Fair; and you shall see, how pleas'd I will be, to

18

languish here; but as you see me decay, (for surely so I shall) do not triumph o're my languid Looks, and laugh at my Pale and meager Face; but, Pitying, say, How easily I might have preserv'd that Face, those Eyes, and all that Youth and Vigour, now no more, from this total Ruine I now behold it in, and love your Slave that dyes, and will be daily and visibly dying, as long as my Eyes can gaze on that fair Object, and my Soul be fed and kept alive with her Charming Wit and Conversation; if Love can live on such Airy Food, (tho' rich in it self, yet unfit, alone, to sustain Life) it shall be for ever dedicated to the lovely *ISABELLA*: But, oh! that time cannot be long! Fate will not lend her Slave many days, who loves too violently, to be satisfy'd to enjoy the fair Object of his Desires, no otherwise than at a *Grate*.'

He ceas'd speaking, for Sighs and Tears stopt his Voice, and he begg'd the liberty to sit down; and his Looks being quite alter'd, *ISABELLA* found her self touch'd to the very Soul, with a concern the most tender, that ever yielding Maid was oppress'd with: She had no power to suffer him to Languish, while she by one soft word could restore him, and being about to say a thousand things that would have been agreeable to him, she saw herself approach'd by some of the *Nuns*, and only had time to say, 'If you love me, live and hope.' The rest of the *Nuns* began to ask *Henault* of News, for he always brought them all that was Novel in the Town, and they were glad still of his Visits, above all other, for they heard, how all Amours and Intrigues pass'd in the World, by this young Cavalier. These last words of *Isabella's* were a Cordial to his Soul, and he, from that, and to conceal the present Affair, endeavour'd to assume all the Gaity he could, and told 'em all he could either remember, or invent, to please 'em, tho' he wish'd them a great way off at that time.

Thus they pass'd the day, till it was a decent hour for him to quit the *Grate*, and for them to draw the Curtain; all that Night did *Isabella* dedicate to Love, she went to Bed, with a Resolution, to think over all she had to do, and to consider, how she should manage this great Affair of her Life: I have already said, she had try'd all that was possible in Human Strength to perform, in the design of quitting a Passion so injurious to her Honour and Virtue, and found no means possible to accomplish it: She had try'd Fasting long, Praying fervently, rigid Penances and Pains, severe Disciplines, all the Mortification, almost to the destruction of Life it self, to conquer the unruly Flame; but still it burnt and rag'd but the more; so, at last, she was forc'd to permit that to conquer her, she could not conquer, and submitted to her Fate, as a thing destin'd her by Heaven it self; and after all this opposition, she fancy'd it was resisting even Divine Providence, to struggle any longer with her Heart; and this being her real Belief, she the more patiently gave way to all the Thoughts that pleas'd her.

As soon as she was laid, without discoursing (as she us'd to do) to *Katteriena*, after they were in Bed, she pretended to be sleepy, and turning from her, setled her self to profound Thinking, and was resolv'd to conclude the Matter, between her Heart, and her Vow of Devotion, that Night, and she, having no more to determine, might end the Affair accordingly, the first opportunity she should have to speak to *Henault*, which was, to fly,

19

and marry him; or, to remain for ever fix'd to her Vow of Chastity. This was the Debate; she brings Reason on both sides: Against the first, she sets the Shame of a Violated Vow, and considers, where she shall shew her Face after such an Action; to the Vow, she argues, that she was born in Sin, and could not live without it; that she was Human, and no Angel, and that, possibly, that Sin might be as soon forgiven, as another; that since all her devout Endeavours could not defend her from the Cause, Heaven ought to execute the Effect; that as to shewing her Face, so she saw that of *Henault* always turned (Charming as it was) towards her with love; what had she to do with the World, or car'd to behold any other?

Some times, she thought, it would be more Brave and Pious to dye, than to break her Vow; but she soon answer'd that, as false Arguing, for Self–Murder was the worst of Sins, and in the Deadly Number. She could, after such an Action, live to repent, and, of two Evils, she ought to chuse the least; she dreads to think, since she had so great a Reputation for Virtue and Piety, both in the *Monastery*, and in the World, what they both would say, when she should commit an Action so contrary to both these, she posest; but, after a whole Night's Debate, Love was strongest, and gain'd the Victory. She never went about to think, how she should escape, because she knew it would be easy, the keeping of the Key of the *Monastery*, [was] often intrusted in her keeping, and was, by turns, in the hands of many more, whose Virtue and Discretion was Infallible, and out of Doubt; besides, her Aunt being the Lady *Abbess*, she had greater privilege than the rest; so that she had no more to do, she thought, than to acquaint *Henault* with her Design, as soon as she should get an opportunity. Which was not quickly; but, in the mean time, *Isabella's* Father dy'd, which put some little stop to our Lover's Happiness, and gave her a short time of Grief; but Love, who, while he is new and young, can do us Miracles, soon wip'd her Eyes, and chas'd away all Sorrows from her Heart, and grew every day more and more impatient, to put her new Design in Execution, being every day more resolv'd. Her Father's Death had remov'd one Obstacle, and secur'd her from his Reproaches; and now she only wants Opportunity, first, to acquaint *Henault*, and then to fly.

She waited not long, all things concurring to her desire; for *Katteriena* falling sick, she had the good luck, as she call'd it then, to entertain *Henault* at the *Grate* oftentimes alone; the first moment she did so, she entertain'd him with the good News, and told him, She had at last vanquish'd her Heart in favour of him, and loving him above all things, Honour, her Vow or Reputation, had resolv'd to abandon her self wholly to him, to give her self up to love and serve him, and that she had no other Consideration in the World; but *Henault*, instead of returning her an Answer, all Joy and Satisfaction, held down his Eyes, and Sighing, with a dejected Look, he cry'd, 'Ah, Madam! Pity a Man so wretched and undone, as not to be sensible of this Blessing as I ought.' She grew pale at this Reply, and trembling, expected he would proceed: "Tis not (continued he) that I want Love, tenderest Passion, and all the desire Youth and Love can inspire; But, Oh, Madam! when I consider, (for raving mad in Love as I am for your sake, I do consider) that if I should take you from this Repose, Nobly Born and Educated, as you are; and, for that Act, should find a rigid Father deprive me of all that ought to support you, and afford your Birth, Beauty, and Merits, their due,

She sacrificed a lot & doesn't feel like he appreciates that.

what would you say? How would you Reproach me?' He sighing, expected her Answer, when Blushes overspreading her Face, she reply'd, in a Tone all haughty and angry, 'Ah, *Henault*! Am I then refus'd, after having abandon'd all things for you? Is it thus, you reward my Sacrific'd Honour, Vows, and Virtue? Cannot you hazard the loss of Fortune to possess *Isabella*, who loses all for you!' Then bursting into Tears, at her misfortune of Loving, she suffer'd him to say, 'Oh, Charming fair one! how industrious is your Cruelty, to find out new Torments for an Heart, already press'd down with the Severities of Love? Is it possible, you can make so unhappy a Construction of the tenderest part of my Passion? And can you imagin it want of Love in me, to consider, how I shall preserve and merit the vast Blessing Heaven has given me? Is my Care a Crime? And would not the most deserving Beauty of the World hate me, if I should, to preserve my Life, and satisfy the Passion of my fond Heart, reduce her to the Extremities of Want and Misery? And is there any thing, in what I have said, but what you ought to take for the greatest Respect and tenderness!' 'Alas! (reply'd *Isabella* sighing) young as I am, all unskilful in Love I find, but what I feel, that Discretion is no part of it; and Consideration, inconsistent with the Nobler Passion, who will subsist of its own Nature, and Love unmixed with any other Sentiment? And 'tis not pure, if it be otherwise: I know, had I mix'd Discretion with mine, my Love must have been less, I never thought of living, but my Love; and, if I consider'd at all, it was, that Grandure and Magnificence were useless Trifles to Lovers, wholly needless and troublesom. I thought of living in some loanly Cottage, far from the noise of crowded busie Cities, to walk with thee in Groves, and silent Shades, where I might hear no Voice but thine; and when we had been tir'd, to sit us done by some cool murmuring Rivulet, and be to each a World, my Monarch thou, and I thy Sovereign Queen, while Wreaths of Flowers shall crown our happy Heads, some fragrant Bank our Throne, and Heaven our Canopy: Thus we might laugh at Fortune, and the Proud, despise the duller World, who place their Joys in mighty Shew and Equipage. Alas! my Nature could not bear it, I am unus'd to Wordly Vanities, and would boast of nothing but my *Henault*; no Riches, but his Love; no Grandure, but his Presence.' She ended speaking, with Tears, and he reply'd, 'Now, now, I find, my *Isabella* loves indeed, when she's content to abandon the World for my sake; Oh! thou hast named the only happy Life that suits my quiet Nature, to be retir'd, has always been my Joy! But to be so with thee! Oh! thou hast charm'd me with a Thought so dear, as has for ever banish'd all my Care, but how to receive thy Goodness! Please think no more what my angry Parent may do, when he shall hear, how I have dispos'd of my self against his Will and Pleasure, but trust to Love and Providence; no more! be gone all Thoughts, but those of *Isabella*!'

As soon as he had made an end of expressing his Joy, he fell to consulting how, and when, she should escape; and since it was uncertain, when she should be offer'd the Key, for she would not ask for it, she resolv'd to give him notice, either by word of Mouth, or a bit of Paper she would write in, and give him through the *Grate* the first opportunity; and, parting for that time, they both resolv'd to get up what was possible for their Support, till Time should reconcile Affairs and Friends, and to wait the happy hour.

21

Isabella's dead Mother had left Jewels, of the value of 2000 *l.* to her Daughter, at her Decease, which Jewels were in the possession, now, of the Lady *Abbess*, and were upon Sale, to be added to the Revenue of the *Monastery*, and as *Isabella* was the most Prudent of her Sex, at least, had hitherto been so esteem'd, she was intrusted with all that was in possession of the Lady *Abbess*, and 'twas not difficult to make her self Mistress of all her own Jewels; as also, some 3 or 400 *l.* in Gold, that was hoarded up in her Ladyship's Cabinet, against any Accidents that might arrive to the *Monastery*; these *Isabella* also made her own, and put up with the Jewels; and having acquainted *Henault*, with the Day and Hour of her Escape, he got together what he could, and waiting for her, with his Coach, one Night, when no body was awake but her self, when rising softly, as she us'd to do, in the Night, to her Devotion, she stole so dexterously out of the *Monastery*, as no body knew any thing of it; she carry'd away the Keys with her, after having lock'd all the Doors, for she was intrusted often with all. She found *Henault* waiting in his Coach, and trusted none but an honest Coachman that lov'd him; he receiv'd her with all the Transports of a truly ravish'd Lover, and she was infinitely charm'd with the new Pleasure of his Embraces and Kisses.

They drove out of Town immediately, and because she durst not be seen in that Habit, (for it had been immediate Death for both) they drove into a Thicket some three Miles from the Town, where *Henault* having brought her some of his younger Sister's Clothes, he made her put off her Habit, and put on those; and, rending the other, they hid them in a Sand-pit, covered over with Broom, and went that Night forty Miles from *Iper*, to a little Town upon the River *Rhine*, where, changing their Names, they were forthwith married, and took a House in a Country Village, a Farm, where they resolv'd to live retir'd, by the name of *Beroone*, and drove a Farming Trade; however, not forgetting to set Friends and Engines at work, to get their Pardon, as Criminals, first, that had trangress'd the Law; and, next, as disobedient Persons, who had done contrary to the Will and Desire of their Parents: *Isabella* writ to her Aunt the most moving Letters in the World, so did *Henault* to his Father; but she was a long time, before she could gain so much as an answer from her Aunt, and *Henault* was so unhappy, as never to gain one from his Father; who no sooner heard the News that was spread over all the Town and Country, that young *Henault* was fled with the so fam'd *Isabella*, a *Nun*, and singular for Devotion and Piety of Life, but he immediately setled his Estate on his younger Son, cutting *Henault* off with all his Birthright, which was 5000 *l.* a Year. This News, you may believe, was not very pleasing to the young Man, who tho' in possession of the loveliest Virgin, and now Wife, that ever Man was bless'd with; yet when he reflected, he should have children by her, and these and she should come to want, (he having been magnificently Educated, and impatient of scanty Fortune) he laid it to Heart, and it gave him a thousand Uneasinesses in the midst of unspeakable Joys; and the more be strove to hide his Sentiments from *Isabella*, the more tormenting it was within; he durst not name it to her, so insuperable a Grief it would cause in her, to hear him complain; and tho' she could live hardly, as being bred to a devout and severe Life, he could not, but must let the Man of Quality shew it self; even in the disguise of an humbler Farmer: Besides all this, he found nothing of his Industry thrive, his Cattel

22

still dy'd in the midst of those that were in full Vigour and Health of other Peoples; his Crops of Wheat and Barly, and other Grain, tho' manag'd by able and knowing Husbandmen, were all, either Mildew'd, or Blasted, or some Misfortune still arriv'd to him; his Coach-Horses would fight and kill one another, his Barns sometimes be fir'd; so that it became a Proverb all over the Country, if any ill Luck had arriv'd to any body, they would say, 'They had Monsieur *BEROONE'S* Luck.' All these Reflections did but add to his Melancholy, and he grew at last to be in some want, insomuch, that *Isabella*, who had by her frequent Letters, and submissive Supplications, to her Aunt, (who lov'd her tenderly) obtain'd her Pardon, and her Blessing; she now press'd her for some Money, and besought her to consider, how great a Fortune she had brought to the *Monastery*, and implor'd, she would allow her some Sallary out of it, for she had been marry'd two Years, and most of what she had was exhausted. The Aunt, who found, that what was done, could not be undone, did, from time to time, supply her so, as one might have liv'd very decently on that very Revenue; but that would not satisfy the great Heart of *Henault*. He was now about three and twenty Years old, and *Isabella* about eighteen, too young, and too lovely a Pair, to begin their Misfortunes so soon; they were both the most Just and Pious in the World; they were Examples of Goodness, and Eminent for Holy Living, and for perfect Loving, and yet nothing thriv'd they undertook; they had no Children, and all their Joy was in each other; at last, one good Fortune arriv'd to them, by the Solicitations of the Lady *Abbess*, and the *Bishop*, who was her near Kinsman, they got a Pardon for *Isabella's* quitting the *Monastery*, and marrying, so that she might now return to her own Country again. *Henault* having also his Pardon, they immediately quit the place, where they had remain'd for two Years, and came again into *Flanders*, hoping, the change of place might afford 'em better Luck.

Henault then began again to solicit his Cruel Father, but nothing would do, he refus'd to see him, or to receive any Letters from him; but, at last, he prevail'd so far with him, as that he sent a Kinsman to him, to assure him, if he would leave his Wife, and go into the *French* Campagn, he would Equip him as well as his Quality requir'd, and that, according as he behav'd himself, he should gain his Favour; but if he liv'd Idly at home, giving up his Youth and Glory to lazy Love, he would have no more to say to him, but race him out of his Heart, and out of his Memory.

He had setled himself in a very pretty House, furnished with what was fitting for the Reception of any Body of Quality that would live a private Life, and they found all the Respect that their Merits deserv'd from all the World, every body entirely loving and endeavouring to serve them; and *Isabella* so perfectly had the Ascendent over her Aunt's Heart, that she procur'd from her all that she could desire, and much more than she could expect. She was perpetually progging and saving all that she could, to enrich and advance her, and, at last, pardoning and forgiving *Henault*, lov'd him as her own Child; so that all things look'd with a better Face than before, and never was so dear and fond a Couple seen, as *Henault* and *Isabella*; but, at last, she prov'd with Child, and the Aunt, who might reasonably believe, so young a Couple would have a great many Children, and foreseeing

23

there was no Provision likely to be made them, unless he pleas'd his Father, for if the Aunt should chance to dye, all their Hope was gone; she therefore daily solicited him to obey his Father, and go to the Camp; and that having atchiev'd Fame and Renown, he would return a Favourite to his Father, and Comfort to his Wife: After she had solicited in vain, for he was not able to endure the thought of leaving *Isabella*, melancholy as he was with his ill Fortune; the *Bishop*, kinsman to *Isabella*, took him to task, and urg'd his Youth and Birth, and that he ought not to wast both without Action, when all the World was employ'd; and, that since his Father had so great a desire he should go into a Campagn, either to serve the *Venetian* against the *Turks*, or into the *French* Service, which he lik'd best; he besought him to think of it; and since he had satisfy'd his Love, he should and ought to satisfy his Duty, it being absolutely necessary for the wiping off the Stain of his Sacrilege, and to gain him the favour of Heaven, which, he found, had hitherto been averse to all he had undertaken: In fine, all his Friends, and all who lov'd him, joyn'd in this Design, and all thought it convenient, nor was he insensible of the Advantage it might bring him; but Love, which every day grew fonder and fonder in his Heart, oppos'd all their Reasonings, tho' he saw all the Brave Youth of the Age preparing to go, either to one Army, or the other.

At last, he lets *Isabella* know, what Propositions he had made him, both by his Father, and his Relations; at the very first Motion, she almost fainted in his Arms, while he was speaking, and it possess'd her with so intire a Grief, that she miscarry'd, to the insupportable Torment of her tender Husband and Lover, so that, to re-establish her Repose, he was forc'd to promise not to go; however, she consider'd all their Circumstances, and weigh'd the Advantages that might redound both to his Honour and Fortune, by it; and, in a matter of a Month's time, with the Persuasions and Reasons of her Friends, she suffer'd him to resolve upon going, her self determining to retire to the *Monastery*, till the time of his Return; but when she nam'd the *Monastery*, he grew pale and disorder'd, and obliged her to promise him, not to enter into it any more, for fear they should never suffer her to come forth again; so that he resolv'd not to depart, till she had made a Vow to him, never to go again within the Walls of a Religious House, which had already been so fatal to them. She promis'd, and he believ'd.

Henault, at last, overcame his Heart, which pleaded so for his Stay, and sent his Father word, he was ready to obey him, and to carry the first Efforts of his Arms against the common Foes of Christendom, the *Turks*; his Father was very well pleas'd at this, and sent him Two thousand Crowns, his Horses and Furniture sutable to his Quality, and a Man to wait on him; so that it was not long e're he got himself in order to be gone, after a dismal parting.

He made what hast he could to the *French* Army, then under the Command of the Monsignior, the Duke of *Beaufort*, then at *Candia*, and put himself a Voluntier under his Conduct; in which Station was *Villenoys*, who, you have already heard, was so passionate a Lover of *Isabella*, who no sooner heard of *Henault's* being arriv'd, and that he was Husband to *Isabella*, but he was impatient to learn, by what strange Adventure he came to

24

gain her, even from her Vow'd Retreat, when he, with all his Courtship, could not be so happy, tho' she was then free in the World, and Unvow'd to Heaven.

As soon as he sent his Name to *Henault*, he was sent for up, for *Henault* had heard of *Villenoys*, and that he had been a Lover of *Isabella*; they receiv'd one another with all the endearing Civility imaginable for the aforesaid Reason, and for that he was his Country-man, tho' unknown to him, *Villenoys* being gone to the Army, just as *Henault* came from the *Jesuits* College. A great deal of Endearment pass'd between them, and they became, from that moment, like two sworn Brothers, and he receiv'd the whole Relation from *Henault*, of his Amour.

It was not long before the Siege began anew, for he arriv'd at the beginning of the Spring, and, as soon as he came, almost, they fell to Action; and it happen'd upon a day, that a Party of some Four hundred Men resolv'd to sally out upon the Enemy, as, when ever they could, they did; but as it is not my business to relate the History of the War, being wholly unacquainted with the Terms of Battels, I shall only say, That these Men were led by *Villenoys*, and that *Henault* would accompany him in this Sally, and that they acted very Noble, and great Things, worthy of a Memory in the History of that Siege; but this day, particularly, they had an occasion to shew their Valour, which they did very much to their Glory; but, venturing too far, they were ambush'd, in the persuit of the Party of the Enemies, and being surrounded, *Villenoys* had the unhappiness to see his gallant Friend fall, fighting and dealing of Wounds around him, even as he descended to the Earth, for he fell from his Horse at the same moment that he kill'd a *Turk*; and *Villenoys* could neither assist him, nor had he the satisfaction to be able to rescue his dead Body from under the Horses, but, with much ado, escaping with his own Life, got away, in spite of all that follow'd him, and recover'd the Town, before they could overtake him: He passionately bewail'd the Loss of this brave young Man, and offer'd any Recompence to those, that would have ventur'd to have search'd for his dead Body among the Slain; but it was not fit to hazard the Living, for unnecessary Services to the Dead; and tho' he had a great mind to have Interr'd him, he rested content with what he wish'd to pay his Friends Memory, tho' he could not: So that all the Service now he could do him, was, to write to *Isabella*, to whom he had not writ, tho' commanded by her so to do, in three Years before, which was never since she took Orders. He gave her an Account of the Death of her Husband, and how Gloriously he fell fighting for the Holy Cross, and how much Honour he had won, if it had been his Fate to have outliv'd that great, but unfortunate, Day, where, with 400 Men, they had kill'd 1500 of the Enemy. The General *Beaufort* himself had so great a Respect and Esteem for this young Man, and knowing him to be of Quality, that he did him the honour to bemoan him, and to send a Condoling Letter to *Isabella*, how much worth her Esteem he dy'd, and that he had Eterniz'd his Memory with the last Gasp of his Life.

When this News arriv'd, it may be easily imagin'd, what Impressions, or rather Ruins, it made in the Heart of this fair Mourner; the Letters came by his Man, who saw him fall in Battel, and came off with those few that escap'd with *Villenoys*; he brought back what

25

Money he had, a few Jewels, with *Isabella's* Picture that he carry'd with him and had left in his Chamber in the Fort at *Candia*, for fear of breaking it in Action. And now *Isabella's* Sorrow grew to the Extremity, she thought, she could not suffer more than she did by his Absence, but she now found a Grief more killing; she hung her Chamber with Black, and liv'd without the Light of Day: Only Wax Lights, that let her behold the Picture of this Charming Man, before which she sacrific'd Floods of Tears. He had now been absent about ten Months, and she had learnt just to live without him, but Hope preserv'd her then; but now she had nothing, for which to wish to live. She, for about two Months after the News arriv'd, liv'd without seeing any Creature but a young Maid, that was her Woman; but extream Importunity oblig'd her to give way to the Visits of her Friends, who endeavour'd to restore her Melancholy Soul to its wonted Easiness; for, however it was oppress'd within, by *Henault's* Absence, she bore it off with a modest Chearfulness; but now she found, that Fortitude and Virtue fail'd her, when she was assur'd, he was no more: She continu'd thus Mourning, and thus inclos'd, the space of a whole Year, never suffering the Visit of any Man, but of a near Relation; so that she acquir'd a Reputation, such as never any young Beauty had, for she was now but Nineteen, and her Face and Shape more excellent than ever; she daily increas'd in Beauty, which, joyn'd to her Exemplary Piety, Charity, and all other excellent Qualities, gain'd her a wonderous Fame, and begat an Awe and Reverence in all that heard of her, and there was no Man of any Quality, that did not Adore her. After her Year was up, she went to the Churches, but would never be seen any where else abroad, but that was enough to procure her a thousand Lovers; and some, who had the boldness to send her Letters, which, if she receiv'd, she gave no Answer to, and many she sent back unread and unseal'd: So that she would encourage none, tho' their Quality was far beyond what she could hope; but she was resolv'd to marry no more, however her Fortune might require it.

It happen'd, that, about this time, *Candia* being unfortunately taken by the *Turks*, all the brave Men that escap'd the Sword, return'd, among them, *Villenoys*, who no sooner arriv'd, but he sent to let *Isabella* know of it, and to beg the Honour of waiting on her; desirous to learn what Fate befel her dear Lord, she suffer'd him to visit her, where he found her, in her Mourning, a thousand times more Fair, (at least, he fancy'd so) than ever she appear'd to be; so that if he lov'd her before, he now ador'd her; if he burnt then, he rages now; but the awful Sadness, and soft Languishment of her Eyes, hinder'd him from the presumption of speaking of his Passion to her, tho' it would have been no new thing; and his first Visit was spent in the Relation of every Circumstance of *Henault's* Death; and, at his going away, he begg'd leave to visit her sometimes, and she gave him permission: He lost no time, but made use of the Liberty she had given him; and when his Sister, who was a great Companion of *Isabella's*, went to see her, he would still wait on her; so that, either with his own Visits, and those of his Sister's, he saw *Isabella* every day, and had the good luck to see, he diverted her, by giving her Relations of Transactions of the Siege, and the Customs and Manners of the *Turks*. All he said, was with so good a Grace, that he render'd every thing agreeable; he was, besides, very Beautiful, well made, of Quality and Fortune, and fit to inspire Love.

He made his Visits so often, and so long, that, at last, he took the Courage to speak of his Passion, which, at first, *Isabella* would by no means hear of, but, by degrees, she yielded more and more to listen to his tender Discourse; and he liv'd thus with her two Years, before he could gain any more upon her Heart, than to suffer him to speak of Love to her; but that, which subdu'd her quite was, That her Aunt, the Lady *Abbess*, dy'd, and with her, all the Hopes and Fortune of *Isabella*, so that she was left with only a Charming Face and Meen, a Virtue, and a Discretion above her Sex, to make her Fortune within the World; into a Religious House, she was resolv'd not to go, because her Heart deceiv'd her once, and she durst not trust it again, whatever it promis'd.

The death of this Lady made her look more favourably on *Villenoys*; but yet, she was resolv'd to try his Love to the utmost, and keep him off, as long as 'twas possible she could subsist, and 'twas for Interest she married again, tho' she lik'd the Person very well; and since she was forc'd to submit her self to be a second time a Wife, she thought, she could live better with *Villenoys*, than any other, since for him she ever had a great Esteem; and fancy'd the Hand of Heaven had pointed out her Destiny, which she could not avoid, without a Crime.

So that when she was again importun'd by her impatient Lover, she told him, She had made a Vow to remain three Years, at least, before she would marry again, after the Death of the best of Men and Husbands, and him who had the Fruits of her early Heart; and, notwithstanding all the Solicitations of *Villenoys*, she would not consent to marry him, till her Vow of Widowhood was expir'd.

He took her promise, which he urg'd her to give him, and to shew the height of his Passion in his obedience; he condescends to stay her appointed time, tho' he saw her every day, and all his Friends and Relations made her Visits upon this new account, and there was nothing talk'd on, but this design'd Wedding, which, when the time was expir'd, was perform'd accordingly with great Pomp and Magnificence, for *Villenoys* had no Parents to hinder his Design; or if he had, the Reputation and Virtue of this Lady would have subdu'd them.

The Marriage was celebrated in this House, where she liv'd ever since her Return from *Germany*, from the time she got her Pardon; and when *Villenoys* was preparing all things in a more magnificent Order at his Villa, some ten Miles from the City, she was very melancholy, and would often say, She had been us'd to such profound Retreat, and to live without the fatigue of Noise and Equipage, that, she fear'd, she should never endure that Grandeur, which was proper for his Quality; and tho' the House, in the Country, was the most beautifully Situated in all *Flanders*, she was afraid of a numerous Train, and kept him, for the most part, in this pretty City Mansion, which he Adorn'd and Enlarg'd, as much as she would give him leave; so that there wanted nothing, to make this House fit to receive the People of the greatest Quality, little as it was: But all the Servants and Footmen, all but one *Valet*, and the Maid, were lodg'd abroad, for *Isabella*, not much us'd to

27

the sight of Men about her, suffer'd them as seldom as possible, to come in her Presence, so that she liv'd more like a *Nun* still, than a Lady of the World; and very rarely any Maids came about her, but *Maria*, who had always permission to come, when ever she pleas'd, unless forbidden.

As *Villenoys* had the most tender and violent Passion for his Wife, in the World, he suffer'd her to be pleas'd at any rate, and to live in what Method she best lik'd, and was infinitely satisfy'd with the Austerity and manner of her Conduct, since in his Arms, and alone, with him, she wanted nothing that could Charm; so that she was esteemed the fairest and best of Wives, and he the most happy of all Mankind. When she would go abroad, she had her Coaches Rich and Gay, and her Livery ready to attend her in all the Splendour imaginable; and he was always buying one rich Jewel, or Necklace, or some great Rarity or other, that might please her; so that there was nothing her Soul could desire, which it had not, except the Assurance of Eternal Happiness, which she labour'd incessantly to gain. She had no Discontent, but because she was not bless'd with a Child; but she submits to the pleasure of Heaven, and endeavour'd, by her good Works, and her Charity, to make the Poor her Children, and was ever doing Acts of Virtue, to make the Proverb good, *That more are the Children of the Barren, than the Fruitful Woman.* She liv'd in this Tranquility, belov'd by all, for the space of five Years, and Time (and perpetual Obligations from *Villenoys*, who was the most indulgent and indearing Man in the World) had almost worn out of her Heart the Thought of *Henault*, or if she remember'd him, it was in her Prayers, or sometimes with a short sigh, and no more, tho' it was a great while, before she could subdue her Heart to that Calmness; but she was prudent, and wisely bent all her Endeavours to please, oblige, and caress, the deserving Living, and to strive all she could, to forget the unhappy Dead, since it could not but redound to the disturbance of her Repose, to think of him; so that she had now transferr'd all that Tenderness she had for him, to *Villenoys*.

Villenoys, of all Diversions, lov'd Hunting, and kept, at his Country House, a very famous Pack of Dogs, which he us'd to lend, sometimes, to a young Lord, who was his dear Friend, and his Neighbour in the Country, who would often take them, and be out two or three days together, where he heard of Game, and oftentimes *Villenoys* and he would be a whole Week at a time exercising in this Sport, for there was no Game near at hand. This young Lord had sent him a Letter, to invite him fifteen Miles farther than his own *Villa*, to hunt, and appointed to meet him at his Country House, in order to go in search of this promis'd Game; So that *Villenoys* got about a Week's Provision, of what Necessaries he thought he should want in that time; and taking only his *Valet*, who lov'd the Sport, he left *Isabella* for a Week to her Devotion, and her other innocent Diversions of fine Work, at which she was Excellent, and left the Town to go meet this young Challenger.

When *Villenoys* was at any time out, it was the custom of *Isabella* to retire to her Chamber, and to receive no Visits, not even the Ladies, so absolutely she devoted her self to her Husband: All the first day she pass'd over in this manner, and Evening being come, she order'd her Supper to be brought to her Chamber, and, because it was Washing-day the next day, she order'd all her Maids to go very early to Bed, that they might be up betimes, and to leave only *Maria* to attend her; which was accordingly done. This *Maria* was a young Maid, that was very discreet, and, of all things in the World, lov'd her Lady, whom she had liv'd with, ever since she came from the *Monastery*.

When all were in Bed, and the little light Supper just carry'd up to the Lady, and only, as I said, *Maria* attending, some body knock'd at the Gate, it being about Nine of the Clock at Night; so *Maria* snatching up a Candle, went to the Gate, to see who it might be; when she open'd the Door, she found a Man in a very odd Habit, and a worse Countenance, and asking, Who he would speak with? He told her, Her Lady: My Lady (reply'd *Maria*) does not use to receive Visits at this hour; Pray, what is your Business? He reply'd, That which I will deliver only to your Lady, and that she may give me Admittance, pray, deliver her this Ring: And pulling off a small Ring, with *Isabella's* Name and Hair in it, he gave it *Maria*, who, shutting the Gate upon him, went in with the Ring; as soon as *Isabella* saw it, she was ready to swound on the Chair where she sate, and cry'd, Where had you this? *Maria* reply'd, An old rusty Fellow at the Gate gave it me, and desired, it might be his Pasport to you; I ask'd his Name, but he said, You knew him not, but he had great News to tell you. *Isabella* reply'd, (almost swounding again) Oh, *Maria!* I am ruin'd. The Maid, all this while, knew not what she meant, nor, that that was a Ring given to *Henault* by her Mistress, but endeavouring to recover her, only ask'd her, What she should say to the old Messenger? *Isabella* bid her bring him up to her, (she had scarce Life to utter these last words) and before she was well recover'd, *Maria* enter'd with the Man; and *Isabella* making a Sign to her, to depart the Room, she was left alone with him.

Henault (for it was he) stood trembling and speechless before her, giving her leisure to take a strict Survey of him; at first finding no Feature nor Part of *Henault* about him, her Fears began to lessen, and she hop'd, it was not he, as her first Apprehensions had suggested; when he (with the Tears of Joy standing in his Eyes, and not daring suddenly to approach her, for fear of encreasing that Disorder he saw in her pale Face) began to speak to her, and cry'd, Fair Creature! is there no Remains of your *Henault* left in this Face of mine, all o'regrown with Hair? Nothing in these Eyes, sunk with eight Years Absence from you, and Sorrows? Nothing in this Shape, bow'd with Labour and Griefs, that can inform you? I was once that happy Man you lov'd! At these words, Tears stop'd his Speech, and *Isabella* kept them Company, for yet she wanted Words. Shame and Confusion fill'd her Soul, and she was not able to lift her Eyes up, to consider the Face of him, whose Voice she knew so perfectly well. In one moment, she run over a thousand Thoughts. She finds, by his Return, she is not only expos'd to all the Shame imaginable; to all the Upbraiding, on his part, when he shall know she is marry'd to another; but all the Fury and Rage of *Villenoys*, and the Scorn of the Town, who will look on her as an Adulteress: She sees *Henault* poor, and knew, she must fall from all the Glory and Tranquility she had for five happy Years triumph'd in; in which time, she had known no Sorrow, or Care, tho' she had endur'd a thousand with *Henault*. She dyes, to think, however, that he should know, she had been so lightly in Love with him, to marry again; and she dyes, to think, that *Villenoys*

29

must see her again in the Arms of *Henault*; besides, she could not recal her Love, for Love, like Reputation, once fled, never returns more. 'Tis impossible to love, and cease to love, (and love another) and yet return again to the first Passion, tho' the Person have all the Charms, or a thousand times more than it had, when it first conquer'd. This Mistery in Love, it may be, is not generally known, but nothing is more certain. One may a while suffer the Flame to languish, but there may be a reviving Spark in the Ashes, rak'd up, that may burn anew; but when 'tis quite extinguish'd, it never returns or rekindles.

'Twas so with the Heart of *Isabella*; had she believ'd, *Henault* had been living, she had lov'd to the last moment of their Lives; but, alas! the Dead are soon forgotten, and she now lov'd only *Villenoys*.

After they had both thus silently wept, with very different sentiments, she thought 'twas time to speak; and dissembling as well as she could, she caress'd him in her Arms, and told him, She could not express her Surprize and Joy for his Arrival. If she did not Embrace him heartily, or speak so Passionately as she us'd to do, he fancy'd it her Confusion, and his being in a condition not so fit to receive Embraces from her; and evaded them as much as 'twas possible for him to do, in respect to her, till he had dress'd his Face, and put himself in order; but the Supper being just brought up, when he knock'd, she order'd him to sit down and Eat, and he desir'd her not to let *Maria* know who he was, to see how long it would be, before she knew him or would call him to mind. But *Isabella* commanded *Maria*, to make up a Bed in such a Chamber, without disturbing her Fellows, and dismiss'd her from waiting at Table. The Maid admir'd, what strange, good, and joyful News, this Man had brought her Mistress, that he was so Treated, and alone with her, which never any Man had yet been; but she never imagin'd the Truth, and knew her Lady's Prudence too well, to question her Conduct. While they were at Supper, *Isabella* oblig'd him to tell her, How he came to be reported Dead; of which, she receiv'd Letters, both from Monsieur *Villenoys*, and the Duke of *Beaufort*, and by his Man the News, who saw him Dead? He told her, That, after the Fight, of which, first, he gave her an account, he being left among the Dead, when the Enemy came to Plunder and strip 'em, they found, he had Life in him, and appearing as an Eminent Person, they thought it better Booty to save me, (continu'd he) and get my Ransom, than to strip me, and bury me among the Dead; so they bore me off to a Tent, and recover'd me to Life; and, after that, I was recover'd of my Wounds, and sold, by the Soldier that had taken me, to a Spahee, who kept me a Slave, setting a great Ransom on me, such as I was not able to pay. I writ several times, to give you, and my Father, an account of my Misery, but receiv'd no Answer, and endur'd seven Years of Dreadful Slavery: When I found, at last, an opportunity to make my Escape, and from that time, resolv'd, never to cut the Hair of this Beard, till I should either see my dearest *Isabella* again, or hear some News of her. All that I fear'd, was, That she was Dead; and, at that word, he fetch'd a deep Sigh; and viewing all things so infinitely more Magnificent than he had left 'em, or, believ'd, she could afford; and, that she was far more Beautiful in Person, and Rich in Dress, than when he left her: He had a thousand Torments of Jealousie that seiz'd him, of which, he durst not make any mention, but rather chose to wait a little, and see, whether she had lost her Virtue: He desir'd, he might send for a Barber, to put his Face in some handsomer Order, and more fit for the Happiness 'twas that Night to receive; but she told him, No Dress, no Disguise, could render him more Dear and Acceptable to her, and that to morrow was time enough, and that his Travels had render'd him more fit for Repose, than Dressing. So that after a little while, they had talk'd over all they had a mind to say, all that was very indearing on his side, and as much Concern as she could force, on hers; she conducted him to his Chamber, which was very rich, and which gave him a very great addition of Jealousie: However, he suffer'd her to help him to Bed, which she seem'd to do, with all the tenderness in the World; and when she had seen him laid, she said, She would go to her Prayers, and come to him as soon as she had done, which being before her usual Custom, it was not a wonder to him she stay'd long, and he, being extreamly tir'd with his Journy, fell asleep. 'Tis true, *Isabella* essay'd to Pray, but alas! it was in vain, she was distracted with a thousand Thoughts what to do, which the more she thought, the more it distracted her: she was a thousand times about to end her Life, and, at one stroke, rid her self of the Infamy, that, she saw, must inevitably fall upon her; but Nature was frail, and the Tempter strong: And after a thousand Convulsions, even worse than Death it self, she resolv'd upon the Murder of *Henault*, as the only means of removing all the obstacles to her future Happiness; she resolv'd on this, but after she had done so, she was seiz'd with so great Horror, that she imagin'd, if she perform'd it, she should run Mad; and yet, if she did not, she should be also Frantick, with the Shames and Miseries that would befal her; and believing the Murder the least Evil, since she could never live with him, she fix'd her Heart on that; and causing her self to be put immediately to Bed, in her own Bed, she made *Maria* go to hers, and when all was still, she softly rose, and taking a Candle with her, only in her Night-Gown and Slippers, she goes to the Bed of the Unfortunate *Henault*, with a Penknife in her hand; but considering, she knew not how to conceal the Blood, should she cut his Throat, she resolves to Strangle him, or Smother him with a Pillow; that last thought was no sooner borne, but put in Execution; and, as he soundly slept, she smother'd him without any Noise, or so much as his Strugling: But when she had done this dreadful Deed, and saw the dead Corps of her once-lov'd Lord, lye Smiling (as it were) upon her, she fell into a Swound with the Horror of the Deed, and it had been well for her she had there dy'd; but she reviv'd again, and awaken'd to more and new Horrors, she flyes all frighted from the Chamber, and fancies, the Phantom of her dead Lord persues her; she runs from Room to Room, and starts and stares, as if she saw him continually before her. Now all that was ever Soft and Dear to her, with him, comes into her Heart, and, she finds, he conquers anew, being Dead, who could not gain her Pity, while Living.

While she was thus flying from her Guilt, in vain, she hears one knock with Authority at the Door: She is now more affrighted, if possible, and knows not whither to fly for Refuge; she fancies, they are already the Officers of Justice, and that Ten thousand Tortures and Wrecks are fastening on her, to make her confess the horrid Murder; the knocking increases, and so loud, that the Laundry Maids believing it to be the Woman that us'd to call them up, and help them to Wash, rose, and, opening the Door, let in *Villenoys*; who having been at his Country *Villa*, and finding there a Footman, instead of his Friend, who waited to tell him, His Master was fallen sick of the Small Pox, and could not wait on him, he took Horse, and came back to his lovely *Isabella*; but running up, as he us'd to do, to her Chamber, he found her not, and seeing a Light in another Room, he went in, but found *Isabella* flying from him, out at another Door, with all the speed she could, he admires at this Action, and the more, because his Maid told him Her Lady had been a Bed a good while; he grows a little Jealous, and persues her, but still she flies; at last he caught her in his Arms, where she fell into a swound, but quickly recovering, he set her down in a Chair, and, kneeling before her, implor'd to know what she ayl'd, and why she fled from him, who ador'd her? She only fix'd a ghastly Look upon him, and said, She was not well: 'Oh! (said he) put not me off with such poor Excuses, *Isabella* never fled from me, when Ill, but came to my Arms, and to my Bosom, to find a Cure; therefore, tell me, what's the matter?' At that, she fell a weeping in a most violent manner, and cry'd, She was for ever undone: He, being mov'd with Love and Compassion, conjur'd her to tell what she ayl'd: 'Ah! (said she) thou and I, and all of us, are undone!' At this, he lost all Patience and rav'd, and cry'd, Tell me, and tell me immediately, what's the matter? When she saw his Face pale, and his Eyes fierce, she fell on her knees, and cry'd, 'Oh! you can never Pardon me, if I should tell you, and yet, alas! I am innocent of Ill, by all that's good, I am.' But her Conscience accusing her at that word, she was silent. If thou art Innocent, said *Villenoys*, taking her up in his Arms, and kissing her wet Face, 'By all that's Good, I Pardon thee, what ever thou hast done.' 'Alas! (said she) Oh! but I dare not name it, 'till you swear.' 'By all that's Sacred, (reply'd he) and by whatever Oath you can oblige me to; by my inviolable Love to thee, and by thy own dear Self, I swear, whate're it be, I do forgive thee; I know, thou art too good to commit a Sin I may not with Honour, pardon.'

With this, and hearten'd by his Caresses, she told him, That *Henault* was return'd; and repeating to him his Escape, she said, She had put him to Bed, and when he expected her to come, she fell on her Knees at the Bedside, and confess'd, She was married to *Villenoys*; at that word (said she) he fetch'd a deep Sigh or two, and presently after, with a very little struggling, dy'd; and, yonder, he lyes still in the Bed. After this, she wept so abundantly, that all *Villenoys* could do, could hardly calm her Spirits; but after, consulting what they should do in this Affair, *Villenoys* ask'd her, Who of the House saw him? She said, Only *Maria*, who knew not who he was; so that, resolving to save *Isabella's* Honour, which was the only Misfortune to come, *Villenoys* himself propos'd the carrying him out to the Bridge, and throwing him into the River, where the Stream would carry him down to the Sea, and lose him; or, if he were found, none could know him. So *Villenoys* took a Candle, and went and look'd on him, and found him altogether chang'd, that no Body would know who he was; he therefore put on his Clothes, which was not hard for him to do, for he was scarce yet cold, and comforting again *Isabella*, as well as he could, he went himself into the Stable, and fetched a Sack, such as they us'd for Oats, a new Sack, whereon stuck a great Needle, with a Pack-thread in it; this Sack he brings into the House, and shews to *Isabella*, telling her, He would put the Body in there, for the better convenience of carrying it on his Back. *Isabella* all this while said but little, but, fill'd with Thoughts all Black and

32

Hellish, she ponder'd within, while the Fond and Passionate *Villenoys* was endeavouring to hide her Shame, and to make this an absolute Secret: She imagin'd, that could she live after a Deed so black, *Villenoys* would be eternal reproaching her, if not with his Tongue, at least with his Heart, and embolden'd by one Wickedness, she was the readier for another, and another of such a Nature, as has, in my Opinion, far less Excuse, than the first; but when Fate begins to afflict, she goes through stitch with her Black Work.

When *Villenoys*, who would, for the Safety of *Isabella's* Honour, be the sole Actor in the disposing of this Body; and since he was Young, Vigorous, and Strong, and able to bear it, would trust no one with the Secret, he having put up the Body, and ty'd it fast, set it on a Chair, turning his Back towards it, with the more conveniency to take it upon his Back, bidding *Isabella* give him the two Corners of the Sack in his Hands; telling her, They must do this last office for the Dead, more, in order to the securing their Honour and Tranquility hereafter, than for any other Reason, and bid her be of good Courage, till he came back, for it was not far to the Bridge, and it being the dead of the Night, he should pass well enough. When he had the Sack on his Back, and ready to go with it, she cry'd, Stay, my Dear, some of his Clothes hang out, which I will put in; and with that, taking the Pack-needle with the Thread, sew'd the Sack, with several strong Stitches, to the Collar of *Villenoy's* Coat, without his perceiving it, and bid him go now; and when you come to the Bridge, (said she) and that you are throwing him over the Rail, (which is not above Breast high) be sure you give him a good swing, least the Sack should hang on any thing at the side of the Bridge, and not fall into the Stream; I'le warrant you, (said *Villenoys*) I know how to secure his falling. And going his way with it, Love lent him Strength, and he soon arriv'd at the Bridge; where, turning his Back to the Rail, and heaving the Body over, he threw himself with all his force backward, the better to swing the Body into the River, whose weight (it being made fast to his Collar) pull'd *Villenoys* after it, and both the live and the dead Man falling into the River, which, being rapid at the Bridge, soon drown'd him, especially when so great a weight hung to his Neck; so that he dy'd, without considering what was the occasion of his Fate.

Isabella remain'd the most part of the Night sitting in her Chamber, without going to Bed, to see what would become of her Damnable Design; but when it was towards Morning, and she heard no News, she put herself into Bed, but not to find Repose or Rest there, for that she thought impossible, after so great a Barbarity as she had committed; No, (said she) it is but just I should for ever wake, who have, in one fatal Night, destroy'd two such Innocents. Oh! what Fate, what Destiny, is mine? Under what cursed Planet was I born, that Heaven it self could not divert my Ruine? It was not many Hours since I thought my self the most happy and blest of Women, and now am fallen to the Misery of one of the worst Fiends of Hell.

Such were her Thoughts, and such her Cryes, till the Light brought on new Matter for Grief; for, about Ten of the Clock, News was brought, that Two Men were found dead in the River, and that they were carry'd to the Town-Hall, to lye there, till they were own'd: Within an hour after, News was brought in, that one of these Unhappy Men was *Villenoys*; his *Valet*, who, all this while, imagin'd him in Bed with his Lady, ran to the Hall, to undeceive the People, for he knew, if his Lord were gone out, he should have been call'd to Dress him; but finding it, as 'twas reported, he fell a weeping, and wringing his Hands, in a most miserable manner, he ran home with the News; where, knocking at his Lady's Chamber Door, and finding it fast lock'd, he almost hop'd again, he was deceiv'd; but *Isabella* rising, and opening the Door, *Maria* first enter'd weeping, with the News, and then brought the *Valet*, to testify the fatal Truth of it. *Isabella*, tho' it were nothing but what she expected to hear, almost swounded in her Chair; nor did she feign it, but felt really all the Pangs of Killing Grief; and was so alter'd with her Night's Watching and Grieving, that this new Sorrow look'd very Natural in her. When she was recover'd, she asked a thousand Questions about him, and question'd the Possibility of it; for (said she) he went out this Morning early from me, and had no signs, in his Face, of any Grief or Discontent. Alas! (said the *Valet*) Madam, he is not his own Murderer, some one has done it in Revenge; and then told her, how he was found fasten'd to a Sack, with a dead strange Man ty'd up within it; and every body concludes, that they were both first murder'd, and then drawn to the River, and thrown both in. At the Relation of this Strange Man, she seem'd more amaz'd than before, and commanding the *Valet* to go to the Hall, and to take Order about the Coroner's sitting on the Body of *Villenoys*, and then to have it brought home: She called *Maria* to her, and, after bidding her shut the Door, she cry'd, Ah, *Maria!* I will tell thee what my Heart imagins; but first, (said she) run to the Chamber of the Stranger, and see, if he be still in Bed, which I fear he is not; she did so, and brought word, he was gone; then (said she) my Forebodings are true. When I was in Bed last night, with *Villenoys* (and at that word, she sigh'd as if her Heart–Strings had broken) I told him, I had lodg'd a Stranger in my House, who was by, when my first Lord and Husband fell in Battel; and that, after the Fight, finding him yet alive, he spoke to him, and gave him that Ring you brought me last Night; and conjur'd him, if ever his Fortune should bring him to *Flanders*, to see me, and give me that Ring, and tell me—(with that, she wept, and could scarce speak) a thousand tender and endearing things, and then dy'd in his Arms. For my dear *Henault's* sake (said she) I us'd him nobly, and dismiss'd you that Night, because I was asham'd to have any Witness of the Griefs I paid his Memory: All this I told to *Villenoys* whom I found disorder'd; and, after a sleepless Night, I fancy he got up, and took this poor Man, and has occasion'd his Death: At that, she wept anew, and *Maria*, to whom, all that her Mistress said, was Gospel, verily believ'd it so, without examining Reason; and *Isabella* conjuring her, since none of the House knew of the old Man's being there, (for Old he appear'd to be) that she would let it for ever be a Secret, and, to this she bound her by an Oath; so that none knowing *Henault*, altho' his Body was expos'd there for three Days to Publick View: When the Coroner had Set on the Bodies, he found, they had been first Murder'd some way or other, and then afterwards tack'd together, and thrown into the River, they brought the Body of *Villenoys* home to his House, where, it being laid on a Table, all the House infinitely bewail'd it; and *Isabella* did nothing but swound away, almost as fast as she recover'd Life; however, she would, to compleat her Misery, be led to see this dreadful Victim of her

Cruelty, and, coming near the Table, the Body, whose Eyes were before close shut, now open'd themselves wide, and fix'd them upon *Isabella*, who, giving a great Schreek, fell down in a swound, and the Eyes clos'd again; they had much ado to bring her to Life, but, at last, they did so, and led her back to her Bed, where she remain'd a good while. Different Opinions and Discourses were made, concerning the opening of the Eyes of the Dead Man, and viewing *Isabella*; but she was a Woman of so admirable a Life and Conversation, of so undoubted a Piety and Sanctity of Living, that not the least Conjecture could be made, of her having a hand in it, besides the improbability of it; yet the whole thing was a Mystery, which, they thought, they ought to look into: But a few Days after, the Body of *Villenoys* being interr'd in a most magnificent manner, and, by Will all he had, was long since setled on *Isabella*, the World, instead of Suspecting her, Ador'd her the more, and every Body of Quality was already hoping to be next, tho' the fair Mourner still kept her Bed, and Languish'd daily.

It happen'd, not long after this, there came to the Town a *French* Gentleman, who was taken at the Siege of *Candia*, and was Fellow-Slave with *Henault*, for seven Years, in *Turky*, and who had escap'd with *Henault*, and came as far as *Liege* with him, where, having some Business and Acquaintance with a Merchant, he stay'd some time; but when he parted with *Henault*, he ask'd him, Where he should find him in *Flanders*? *Henault* gave him a Note, with his Name, and Place of Abode, if his Wife were alive; if not, to enquire at his Sister's, or his Father's. This *French* Man came at last, to the very House of *Isabella*, enquiring for this Man, and receiv'd a strange Answer, and was laugh'd at; He found, that was the House, and that the Lady; and enquiring about the Town, and speaking of *Henault's* Return, describing the Man, it was quickly discover'd, to be the same that was in the Sack: He had his Friend taken up (for he was buried) and found him the same, and, causing a *Barber* to Trim him, when his bushy Beard was off, a great many People remember'd him; and the *French* Man affirming, he went to his own Home, all *Isabella's* Family, and her self, were cited before the Magistrate of Justice, where, as soon as she was accus'd, she confess'd the whole Matter of Fact, and, without any Disorder, deliver'd her self in the Hands of Justice, as the Murderess of two Husbands (both belov'd) in one Night: The whole World stood amaz'd at this; who knew her Life a Holy and Charitable Life, and how dearly and well she had liv'd with her Husbands, and every one bewail'd her Misfortune, and she alone was the only Person, that was not afflicted for her self; she was Try'd, and Condemn'd to lose her Head; which Sentence, she joyfully receiv'd, and said, Heaven, and her Judges, were too Merciful to her, and that her Sins had deserv'd much more.

While she was in Prison, she was always at Prayers, and very Chearful and Easie, distributing all she had amongst, and for the Use of, the Poor of the Town, especially to the Poor Widows; exhorting daily, the Young, and the Fair, that came perpetually to visit her, never to break a Vow: for that was first the Ruine of her, and she never since prosper'd, do whatever other good Deeds she could. When the day of Execution came, she appear'd on the Scaffold all in Mourning, but with a Meen so very Majestick and Charming, and a Face so surprizing Fair, where no Languishment or Fear appear'd, but all Chearful as a Bride, that she set all Hearts a flaming, even in that mortifying Minute of Preparation for Death: She made a Speech of half an Hour long, so Eloquent, so admirable a warning to the *Vow-Breakers*, that it was as amazing to hear her, as it was to behold her.

After she had done with the help of *Maria*, she put off her Mourning Vail, and, without any thing over her Face, she kneel'd down, and the Executioner, at one Blow, sever'd her Beautiful Head from her Delicate Body, being then in her Seven and Twentieth Year. She was generally Lamented, and Honourably Bury'd.

FINIS.

Printed in Great Britain
by Amazon

85563646R00031